FICTION HOUSE PRESS
PRESENTS

MIKE SHAYNE
MYSTERY MAGAZINE

September 1959
Vol. 5, No. 4

I0675596

ISBN 978-1-64720-474-7

www.FictionHousePress.com
fictionhousepress@gmail.com

MIKE SHAYNE
MYSTERY MAGAZINE

SEPTEMBER, 1959   Vol. 5, No. 4

NEW FULL-LENGTH MIKE SHAYNE NOVEL
DIE LIKE A DOG
by BRETT HALLIDAY

In all of his experience Mike had never before encountered a murder case quite so bizarre, with so many dark angles and nightmare possibilities. And there was a danger at its core which struck very close to home—with real shock impact.

COMPLETE DETECTIVE NOVELET

SHORT STORIES

LEO MARGULIES
          Publisher

CYLVIA KLEINMAN
          Editorial Director

WALTER P. DALLAS
          Production

MIKE SHAYNE MYSTERY MAGAZINE, Vol. 5, No. 4. Published monthly by RENOWN PUBLICATIONS, INC., 501 Fifth Avenue, N. Y. 17. Subscriptions, 12 issues $4.00; single copies 35¢. Entered as Second Class matter at the post office, New York, N. Y. Additional entry at Concord, N. H. Places and characters in this magazine are wholly fictitious. © 1959 by RENOWN PUBLICATIONS, INC. All rights reserved. September, 1959. Printed in the United States of America. Postmaster—return 3579 to 501 Fifth Ave., N.Y. 17, N.Y.

"I Like Mike!"

So Say the 20,000,000 Devoted

Readers of the Miami Sleuth's

Books. You Can Be 20,000,001!

If you are one of the 20,000,000 Shayne addicts, you have followed the tough, generous, hardhitting, warm-hearted redhead's adventures just about in every medium of modern mass entertainment. You have seen Mike in the movies—heard him on the air, radio and T.V. And you have bought the books—hard-cover and paperbacks—in which Mike has thus far appeared at a clip of almost a million copies apiece. Now, in our magazine you get a *brand-new* Mike Shayne novelet in every issue. No other magazine in America can say that!

On your regular murder-watching jaunt with Mike Shayne, you will encounter the hard-boiled, the refined, the psychological, the detective puzzle—everything, in short or in long, from the bullet in the belly to the sealed room! If it's crime and good fiction, it's for Mike Shayne—so take a walk with the redhead every thirty days—or longer—by making use of the conveniently placed coupon below.

THE NEW MIKE SHAYNE NOVEL

DIE LIKE A DOG

The death of a dog doesn't often play a major role in a murder case. But Mike had a hunch that poison and a house of mourning were just parts of a deadly package deal.

by BRETT HALLIDAY

THERE WAS A QUIZZICAL SMILE on Lucy Hamilton's lips and a little dancing light in her brown eyes as she opened the door to her employer's private office and announced demurely: "There is a lady to see you, Mr. Shayne. A Miss Henrietta Rogell."

It was a warm Miami morning, and Michael Shayne was slumped in a swivel chair behind his wide desk in shirt-sleeves, with collar unbuttoned and tie awry. In front of him was an open checkbook, a

pile of cancelled checks and the monthly bank statement.

"She is John Rogell's sister . . . and only living relative," Lucy added, in response to Mike's questioning stare.

"The millionaire who died a couple of days ago?" Shayne shrugged, closed the checkbook and shoved it aside. "All right, Miss Hamilton. Show her in."

Shayne got to his feet behind the desk when Lucy ushered the prospective client into his office a

5

few moments later. Miss Rogell looked to be a tough seventy. She was tall and angular, and had a seamed face that had the color and appearance of old leather. Brown hair that was liberally streaked with gray was drawn back tightly from her face into an untidy bun. She wore a gray silk suit with pleated skirt, and loose jacket that hung awkwardly from bony shoulders.

Lucy said, "This is Miss Henrietta Rogell, Mr. Shayne," and went out, closing the door to the private office.

Miss Rogell's voice matched her appearance. It was strong and deep without being harsh or masculine. She lowered herself solidly into the chair and planted both feet flat in front of her with knees together.

"Now then," she said. "Before I waste any more of my time, I want to know exactly what your charges are."

Shayne sat down in his swivel chair and leaned back comfortably. "My charges for what?"

"For whatever you do. Detecting, of course. You do call yourself a detective, I believe. Let's have it understood from the beginning so there'll be no outrageous bill for me to pay at the end. Exactly what do you consider your time worth?"

Shayne got a pack of cigarettes from his shirt pocket and lit one. He blew out the match with a stream of smoke and said, "That depends entirely on what I am able to do for you. I think you've come to the wrong office, Miss Rogell," he went on briskly before she could speak. "My secretary can give you a list of half a dozen competent detectives who will quote you a flat daily rate for their services . . . plus expenses . . . and they won't pad the expense account too heavily. I think you'd be happier with one of them."

He put his hands flat on the desk in front of him and half rose from his chair. "My secretary will give you that list of names on your way out."

She remained firmly seated and said, "Humph. I like plain speaking, young man. I'm a plain-spoken person myself. I want you to prove that my brother was murdered and to see that the person or persons responsible are made to pay for the crime."

Shayne hesitated, narrowing his eyes thoughtfully, and then sank back into his chair. "I understood from the newspapers that your brother died of a heart attack."

"Of course. That's what they called it. But I know John was poisoned."

"How do you know?"

"Because I have eyes to see what's going on, and a brain to add two and two together. If I had the proof I wouldn't be here in your office, obviously. That's what I'm hiring you for."

Shayne said, "Murder is a matter for the police, Miss Rogell. Have you discussed your suspicions with them?"

"Do I look like a complete nincompoop? Of course I have. I called the police immediately after John died, and the two detectives who came just listened to me politely and promised they would investigate. Investigate?" Her upper lip curled bitterly over the word. "They asked a few questions of the very people who fed John the poison, and then went away saying they would file a report."

"Did they?"

"I suppose they did, and I'd give a great deal to see just what sort of report they filed. I think it's my right to see it, and I demanded a look at it from Chief Gentry just an hour ago. Oh, I could tell just what he was thinking while he sat there on his fat behind in that plushy office that we taxpayers support. He thinks I'm an hysterical old female with a persecution complex. But how does he explain the fact that the dog died in convulsions after eating the food that had been poisoned for *my* special benefit? How do you think he explains that?"

Shayne said politely, "I have no idea. I do know Will Gentry quite well, and he's an efficient and honest police officer."

"None of them will listen to me," she said grimly. "They all listen to that simpering hussy who married John for his money, and to her paramour who signed the death certificate."

"For the dog?" asked Shayne with interest.

"Of course not for the dog. For John. That young whipper-snapper *she* brought in and foisted on my brother after old Doctor Jenson died two months ago. I warned John against him, but he wouldn't listen to me. Oh, no! The only person he listened to was Anita."

"The death certificate?" said Shayne patiently. "Did it specifically state a heart attack?"

"Naturally. What else would you expect a widow's lover to say about her husband's death? Would you expect *him* to suggest an autopsy . . . knowing full well it must be poison?"

"Let's get back to the dog," said Shayne patiently. "When did it die . . . and how did it come to eat your food?"

"Because I fed it to him out of my plate, that's why." Henrietta Rogell's voice was grimly triumphant. "At supper last night. After I had spoken my mind to them plainly, and I could see they were frightened. I told them right out that I knew John had been poisoned by one or all of them, and I intended to prove it. I warned them I was going to force an autopsy on John before he was cremated tomorrow, and I could see they were frightened. So I had this premonition when the buffet supper was served.

"It was such a perfect opportunity to get rid of me that I was suspicious from the first. And when I tasted my creamed chicken I *knew*. And I slipped some on a saucer to her nasty little dog and he lapped it up. And ten minutes later he was dead. And your efficient and honest chief of police says *that's* no proof," she went on bitterly. "Just a coincidence, he says . . . or an accident. And he says his hands are tied because the chicken was all thrown down the garbage disposal and there's nothing left to analyze. Why not the dog? I asked him.

"And I ask you. Wouldn't *that* be proof that they tried to kill me? But dear little Daffy is already buried and can't be disturbed. Why not? Because he was the darling of Anita's heart and she just can't bear to think of his sacred remains being desecrated by some bad, old doctor making a stomach analysis. And your Will Gentry says he can't legally do a thing if she refuses permission to dig him up."

When she stopped long enough to catch her breath, Shayne said mildly, "Let's go back to supper last night and exactly what happened. You spoke of *them* several times . . . saying you warned them you were planning to have

an autopsy on your brother before his body is cremated. Exactly who is 'them'?"

"Anita and that no-good brother of hers, and Harold Peabody and Dr. Evans," she said promptly. "I'm sure they're all in it together. That is, I think Harold planned it all and put her up to it . . . and then with Doctor Evans twisted around her little finger the way he is, it was in the cards for him to cover up for her.

"And I wouldn't be surprised if that chauffeur and Mrs. Blair were mixed up in it too," she added darkly. "The way I've seen Anita looking at the chauffeur and rubbing against him when she thought nobody was looking. And even Mrs. Blair is changed since John married her. I always thought that she and John . . . well." She shook her head and shrugged and continued briskly:

"So I made sure all of them were there when I told them right out that the wool wasn't pulled over my eyes. Those four sitting there guzzling John's liquor with his funeral tomorrow, and Mrs. Blair coming in and out from the kitchen fixing the table, and Charles lolling out in the kitchen listening to every word that was said. Any one of those six could have slipped the poison into my little chafing dish of creamed chicken because they were all having a casserole of curried shrimp and I'm allergic to seafood and every one of them knew the creamed chicken was just for me and no one else would touch it. So it was safe enough, and I wouldn't be here to tell you about it if I hadn't thought to try it out on her dog first."

"And you say all the rest of the special dish prepared for you was disposed of after the dog died?" Shayne asked with interest.

"You can be sure of that. By the time I called the police, and the detectives got there . . . not a smidgen of chicken left. Not even the pot it was cooked in. All washed clean as a whistle. And the dog already taken out by Charles to be buried, so the detectives couldn't even look at it. And *still* your chief of police can't see anything suspicious in all that. And if something isn't done by this time tomorrow, by the funeral, it'll be just too late. Because John will be burned up and there'll never be any proof he was poisoned by the woman he married and the men she's been carrying on with right under his nose in his own house. They'll all be beyond the law."

"Will Gentry," said Shayne thoughtfully, "is hedged in by a lot of official rules and regulations. Even though he were personally suspicious, there's hardly any official action he could take."

"But you're not," she said tensely.

"I'm not hedged in by anything

except my own conscience," he conceded with a wry grin.

"Chief Gentry intimated as much . . . when he advised me to consult a private detective if I wasn't satisfied with the official investigation made by his men."

"Gentry sent you to me?" Shayne asked in surprise.

"Not in so many words. I did ask him to recommend a private detective and he refused. But I've read about some of your cases, of course, in the papers, and when I asked him pointblank whether even half of the things they say about you are true, he laughed and said just about half. But I got the impression he would be personally pleased if I did come here."

"We have worked together in the past," Shayne agreed. He leaned forward to mash out the very short butt of his cigarette in a tray, and asked abruptly: "Exactly what do you want me to do, Miss Rogell?"

"Why . . . it seems obvious to me. Have the dog's body dissected and analyzed at once. Even Chief Gentry agreed with me that if it were proven my creamed chicken was poisoned he would feel that was sufficient evidence for ordering an autopsy on John."

"You say the dog is already buried?"

"Oh, yes. Anita saw to that. She had Charles remove it at once and take it out to bury it on the grounds. Last night while the detectives were there, they asked Charles where the grave was, and he refused to tell them after Anita ordered him not to. I really think the detectives would have dug it up for examination if they'd known where to find it, but I guess they felt they had no authority to force him to tell them."

"Neither have I," said Shayne bluntly. "Without the dog's body, I don't see what I can do."

"Find it," she shot at him grimly.

Shayne shrugged. "It may be difficult . . . particularly if the chauffeur is as intimate with Mrs. Rogell as you imply."

"Take my word for it, he is," she told him sharply. "But finding the day-old grave of a little dog on the grounds of our estate should not be a superhuman task."

Shayne grinned at her suddenly and rumpled his red hair. There was something damned likable about the old girl and her unshakeable convictions. He said cheerfully, "All right. I'll start detecting. But there's the small matter of a retainer first."

"How small a matter?" she demanded, gimlet-eyed.

"Say five hundred. You can leave a check with my secretary on your way out."

Her clear, blue gaze locked with his for a number of seconds. Then she arose composedly and said, "I will be happy to leave a check with your secretary."

Shayne arose with her. "One final thing," he said as she neared the door. "If you're serious in believing someone at the Rogell house tried to poison you yesterday, I'd move out of the house fast."

She turned with her hand on the knob and smiled for the first time since she had entered his office. It was a wintry smile, but a smile none-the-less. "I am not a complete fool, Mr. Shayne. I took that elementary precaution last night. For the time being, I am occupying a suite at the Waldorf Towers. Where I shall remain until I can return to the house I have lived in for thirty years without fear for my life." She opened the door and went out with a queer sort of dignity in her mannish stride.

Shayne frowned and went thoughtfully to the water cooler where he withdrew two paper cups and nested them inside each other. Then he opened the second drawer of a steel filing cabinet and lifted out a bottle of cognac, wrestled the cork out with his teeth and poured a moderate portion of amber fluid into the inner cup.

Lucy Hamilton came through the door with flushed cheeks as he returned to his desk and took a tentative, pleasurable sip of cognac.

"I took notes over the intercom, Michael. Why did you insist that she give you such a large retainer? Do you realize it practically broke her heart to write that check? I don't see how you think you're going to find a dog's grave on the Rogell estate. Do you realize it's a huge place? Ten or fifteen acres along Brickel Boulevard?"

Shayne said equably, "Five hundred bucks was one way of finding out whether she really believes all the stuff she told me. Get Will Gentry on the phone, angel, and I've got a strange hunch you're going to be the one who finds the dog."

"Me? Michael Shayne! If you think I'm going to go out . . ."

He cut off her indignant response with a negligent wave of his hand. "Let me talk to Will first."

II

WHEN THE CHIEF'S heavy voice rumbled over the wire, Shayne said pleasantly, "Hi, Will. How big a cut do you expect out of my fee from Miss Rogell?"

Will Gentry chuckled, "So the old girl came to you, did she?"

"After our tax-paid police force turned her down. What *is* the dope . . . confidentially?"

"Are you actually taking her case?"

"I've got her check for five C's as a retainer," Shayne told him equably.

"Did she bleed while she wrote it?"

"I gather she does hate to part with money," said Shayne cautiously. "But, damn it, Will, I sort of like the old biddy. Give me the dope on her brother's death."

"There just isn't anything to go on, Mike. We checked it out from A to Z. John Rogell was sixty-eight years old and has had a serious heart condition for years. Been under the care of Doctor Caleb Jenson for many years until the doc kicked off himself a couple months ago. Since then, a Doctor Albert Evans has been seeing the old boy twice a week. Evans has a good reputation, and he signed the death certificate without the slightest hesitation."

"Henrietta says he's in love with the widow. Do you think there's any truth in that?" asked Shayne equably.

"I don't know," Gentry replied. "I haven't met the girl." Gentry paused, and went on more seriously, "Donovan and Petrie covered the whole deal. They do say the girl is put together right and has what looks like hot lips and a roving smile. But, hell! She's in her early twenties and Rogell was sixty-eight. If she was two-timing him the pattern wouldn't have been a too unusual one."

"You mean she might be eager to be rid of him so she could take on a younger man like Doctor Evans," said Shayne promptly.

"Sure, there's that. Or the chauffeur or even Harold Peabody who are both on Henrietta's list. But I tell you, Mike, we checked every angle. I had Doc Higgins go over the complete record of the Rogell case in Jenson's files. And Jenson's secretary told him privately that Jenson had urged Rogell not to marry . . . had predicted that just this would happen if he took on a twenty-three-year-old bride who wasn't exactly on the frigid side."

"You mean Jenson warned him his heart wouldn't stand it."

"Exactly."

"Then maybe Anita did kill him," said Shayne thoughtfully. "If she knew how serious his con-dition was and kept egging him on beyond his physical ability."

"Maybe she did," agreed Gentry. "It wouldn't surprise me one damned bit. But that's not a crime, Mike. Not according to the statutes, it isn't."

"All right, I understand why you passed up Henrietta's accusations after John's death. But what about last night? The little dog that died after he ate her creamed chicken. That looks pretty clear-cut to me."

"Sure it does, hearing Henrietta tell it. But the dog had been pretty sick a couple days ago. Did she tell you that? In fact, it was one of those inbred, pampered little bitches that was always having stomach upsets."

"But it never died of convulsions before, ten minutes after eating a plate of creamed chicken."

"No, it never did," agreed Gentry promptly. "And I'd run a test fast enough if I had the body. But I haven't. It was already buried by the time Donovan and Petrie got to the house."

"A suspicious circumstance in itself," Shayne pointed out. "Why the unseemly hurry?"

"Sure, it's suspicious. On the other hand, there was Anita having hysterics all over the place because of her little pet's death, and her almost pathological horror of any sort of corpse. That's why she urged her husband to put a clause in his will that he should be cremated, and why she hysterically ordered the chauffeur to bury Daffy within minutes after her death."

"So it was Anita who urged Rogell to put a cremation clause in his will?"

"She doesn't deny it. She has a similar clause in her own will."

"I still think the dog should be dug up and analyzed."

"So do I," agreed Gentry promptly. "Give mè proof that the creamed chicken killed her and I'll get an autopsy on Rogell."

"It still seems like a police job to me, Will. You've got the authority to demand that the dog be produced."

Chief Gentry sighed strongly and said, "Listen, Mike. John Rogell was a multi-millionaire and a very important citizen in Miami. His widow is now a multi-millionaire and a very important citizen. There's a certain limit on just how drastic you can be when you're on legal ground that's a little shaky to begin with."

After he hung up the redhead sat for a moment, tugging thoughtfully at his left earlobe, and then opened a drawer of his desk to lift out a Classified Telephone Directory. He settled back and turned the pages slowly, wondering what alphabetical listing to look under. After a couple of false attempts, he found the listing he wanted and made a notation of the address. Then he got up briskly and

went to the outer office where he lifted down his Panama from a rack near the door and glanced at his watch.

"I have to go out for an hour or so," he told Lucy at her desk behind the low railing. "Grab some lunch while I'm gone and be back by one-thirty or two. I expect to have a very important assignment for you."

"Now, if you expect me to go out digging up dead dogs, Michael Shayne . . ." she began stormily, but he interrupted her with a briskly reproving, "You know I wouldn't ask you to do anything like that, angel."

SHAYNE WAS ABSENT for a little more than two hours. Lucy was typing a letter when he returned, and he paused at the railing to ask, "Had your lunch?"

She nodded and he said, "Come in my office a moment."

When Lucy entered, he seated her firmly in the client's chair beside his desk and drew a beautifully printed, four-color, four page brochure from his pocket. He placed it in front of Lucy and leaned over her shoulder to look down at it admiringly.

The cover was done in soft pastel colors. It showed a beautiful blue Persian cat on one side, facing a proud, black French Poodle on the other. Between the two animals was an archway of weathered gray stone with an orange sunburst glowing through it form a distance. Neatly lettered on the archway were the words: PET HAVEN ETERNAL—*Miami's Most Beautiful and Most Exclusive Pet Cemetery.*

Lucy looked at it wonderingly, caught her lower lip between her teeth and glanced up at him. "What on earth, Michael?"

"Don't you think Anita Rogell might find this brochure completely fascinating?" Shayne asked.

"Well . . . from what Henrietta said about her . . ." Lucy paused uneasily, studying Shayne's bland expression. "You mean you think she might be persuaded to have her beloved Daffy disinterred and moved to this morbidly repulsive place?"

Shayne shrugged and said, "Seems reasonable. And I think you're the one to persuade her."

"Me? Now see here, Michael . . ."

"All in the interest of justice," he told her soothingly. "If her Peke wasn't poisoned, what's the harm? The little darling ends up at *Haven Eternal* in much nicer surroundings than she has at present. According to the brochure she can even be cremated if Anita wants that . . . *after* her stomach contents have been analyzed. Sure, you can do it, angel. You look the part okay. Just memorize a few of the salient points in that brochure, and work out a sales pitch. Notice the place on

Page Three where it says they are so discreet that a private car will call if desired, and an attendant in plain business suit will see to removing the remains of the departed pet.

"That's me," he explained with a grin. "I'll turn up with a shovel as soon as you phone me that it's all set. Here, I got this made for you," he went on persuasively, opening his wallet and extracting a freshly printed business card. In large Gothic type, it said *Pet Haven Eternal* and in small type in the lower left hand corner it said: *Miss Lucy Hamilton.*

"This should get you in to see the grieving widow," he told her briskly. "From then on it should be duck soup for a gal of your talents."

Lucy Hamilton shook her head, fluffing out her hair angrily. "Michael Shayne! You're the darndest guy. Why I keep on working for you . . ."

"Because you love it," he laughed at her. "You know you wouldn't pass up this opportunity for anything."

His genial banter eased the anger out of Lucy's eyes.

"But how will I explain that I know about Daffy?"

"There was a small item in the paper about it," Shayne said. "Gentry mentioned that on the phone, along with the rest of our talk. It's a perfect excuse. Hell, if the *Haven Eternal* people were on their toes they'd already have contacted her. Let's hope they've not."

III

A LONG CURVING macadamized drive led off Brickel Avenue through beautifully landscaped grounds to the turreted mansion that John Rogell had built on the bayfront more than thirty years before. It was constructed of rough slabs of native limestone, aged and weathered by the years and the tropical sun. A rakish two-toned convertible and a sleek, black Thunderbird were parked under the long *porte-cochère,* and Lucy Hamilton pulled her light sedan up behind them.

She drew in a deep breath with palpable effort, slowly expelled it, then unlatched the door at her left and picked up her bag. She circled between her car and the rear of the Thunderbird to wide and worn stone steps leading up to a white-columned verandah running the full length of the front of the house. She crossed weathered boards to the double oak doors and put the tip of her forefinger firmly on the electric button.

A full minute went by before the right hand door swung open silently. A sullen-faced maid stood on the threshold of a long, dim hallway facing her. The girl wore a neat, black uniform with white lace at the wrists and neck, and

she had pouting lips and wary eyes.

She said, "What is it, Ma'm?" in a sing-song voice that contrived to convey a faint impression of insolence.

Lucy said, "I'd like a moment with Mrs. Rogell."

The maid tightened her lips momentarily and said, "Madame is not at home to anyone."

Lucy smiled pleasantly and said, "I think she'll see me," with a lot more assurance than she felt. She unsnapped her bag and took out the cardcase, extracted the square of white cardboard and offered it to the maid. "Please take her my card."

For an instant the maid hesitated. Finally she nodded and stepped back, aside to an archway with drawn *portières,* drawing them aside a little ungraciously.

"You can wait in here until I see if Madam can spare you a moment."

Lucy went in to a large, square, sombre room lined with dark walnut bookshelves laden with books in dark leather bindings. There were massive leather chairs in the room, and a man stood in the far corner with his back turned to her. He was bent over a portable bar, and Lucy heard the clink of a swizzle-stick against glass. He wore light tan slacks and a red and yellow plaid sport jacket, and when he swung about to face Lucy with a highball glass in his hand she saw he was a fair-haired young man of about thirty with a wispy mustache and suspiciously high color in his cheeks for a man of his age.

He smiled quickly, showing slightly protruding upper teeth, and exclaimed, "By Jove, there. You've arrived just in the nick of time to save me from a fate worse than death. Drinking alone, you know? And long before the sun has swung over the yard-arm." His voice was thin and a trifle high, but he exuded friendliness like a stray mongrel who has just received his first kind word in weeks.

He advanced toward Lucy, his smile becoming a beaming welcome. "Whatever you're selling, I'll take a lot of. Provided, of course, that you have a drink with me first. My name's Marvin Dale, you know. How long has it been since anyone has told you how gorgeous you are?"

Lucy struggled with a desire to giggle. This must be the ne'er-do-well brother Henrietta had mentioned so disparagingly, and Shayne had told her to keep her eyes open and learn as much about the different members of the family as she could. Dale, she realized, was already slightly drunk as well as being more than slightly amorous, and she decided to indulge him to the extent of one small drink.

"If you could make me a gin and tonic," she agreed hesitantly. "A very light one. I have a business matter to discuss with your sister," she added as stiffly as she could.

Marvin beamed at her as he whisked a gin bottle from a shelf beneath the bar, and opened an ice bucket to deposit two cubes in a tall glass.

"No sense then in holding back on the intake," he said. "If you hope to discuss business with my dear sister today, you may as well relax and have a decent slug."

"I'll settle for this one," Lucy told him, retreating to the depths of a leather-upholstered chair. "I know Mr. Rogell's funeral is tomorrow and I don't like to intrude on her grief. But I did hope to have a moment of her time today."

"Oh, it isn't dear John she's grieving about," Marvin told her with a tight, unpleasant smile. "We've all been expecting that for months. It's her darling Daffy."

"Her Pekinese?" queried Lucy.
"Sombre Daffodil Third."

"That's right, Sombre Daffodil Third," he agreed, taking a gulp of his drink and slouching into another leather chair near Lucy's with both long legs draped over one arm of it. "Why not try this position?" he demanded suddenly with something very close to a leer. "It's the only comfortable way to sit in one of these chairs."

."And not very ladylike." said

Lucy primly, taking a sip of her mild drink.

"Who asked you to be lady-like?" His leer became more pronounced. "You know what the male cricket said to the female grasshopper?"

"No," said Lucy. "I don't know and I'm not interested."

"Well, he said . . . Oh, I say," Marvin interrupted himself as the maid entered through the *portières*, "do you have to intrude just now, Maybelle? Miss Hamilton and I are just getting cozy over a drink and I was about to tell her a very funny story."

Lucy got to her feet quickly and set the glass down as she faced the girl questioningly.

Maybelle made the pretense of a curtsy and said, "Madame will see you in her upstairs sitting room, Ma'm."

Lucy followed her out quickly without looking back at Marvin. The maid led her down the vaulted hallway to a wide stairway curving upward to the right, and up the stairs to another wide hallway where she knocked lightly on a closed door before opening it and announcing, "Miss Hamilton."

The boudoir was chintzy and feminine, and the temperature was like that of a hothouse devoted to the propagation of tropical flowers in contrast to the pleasant coolness of the rest of the big, stone house.

And the girl-woman facing Lucy, propped up against fluffy, silken pillows on a *chaise-longue* was not unlike a rare orchid. There was a look of cultivated fragility, of almost ethereal beauty, in the delicate, finely-drawn features of Anita Rogell. Her violet eyes appeared enormous and had a look of haunting melancholy about them which, Lucy realized on closer inspection, had been artfully attained by the skillful use of purple eyeshadow combined with a dusting of gold powder on carefully shaped brows. Her hair, tightly drawn back from cameo-like features, was the exact color and texture of cornsilk with the morning sun glinting on it, and it displayed a wide forehead and tiny, shell-like ears that lay flat against her head.

Only the mouth was a discordant note in the carefully-wrought perfection of Anita Rogell's face, and the shock-effect of that feature, Lucy knew immediately, had been carefully and unerringly calculated as a vivid contrast with the overall effect.

It was a large, coarse mouth with full, pouting underlip daringly accentuated with heavy lipstick that had a violent orange tinge. It was hard to describe the effect that garish mouth had against the background of cold fragility that was the dominant characteristic of Anita's face. It was a bold and shameless promise of fire and lust that lay beneath the otherwise placid exterior, a flagrant and provocative flaunting of sexual precocity which would have remained otherwise concealed.

At least, that's the way it struck Lucy as she stepped into the overheated room. She had no way of knowing how it would appear to a man who looked at Anita for the first time, and the fleeting thought crossed her mind that she would give a great deal to get Michael Shayne's reaction to the woman in front of her.

But she said composedly, "I apologize for intruding like this, Mrs. Rogell, but when we at *Haven Eternal* learned of your bereavement we felt morally obligated to bring to your attention certain of our unique services which have lessened the pangs of grief of other pet-owners and which we sincerely hope will partially assuage your own."

When Anita merely stared in bewilderment Lucy said quickly: "Wait. Hold on. This little booklet will explain much better than I can if I talked for hours." She opened her bag and extracted the brochure. "It will only take a moment of your time to glance through it and determine which of our services you feel would be most suitable to assure your dear Sombre Daffodil Third that final peace and utter tranquility that every owner of a four-footed friend who was so devoted in life

must desire for the canine soul that has passed onward over the Great Divide to enter the realm of peace that passeth understanding."

Lucy noticed a peculiarly wary, almost frightened glint in Anita's eyes as she completed this remarkable speech and pressed the booklet into the woman's somewhat reluctant hands, and she thought, "Oh dear. Did I overdue it that time? I don't think this gal is as dumb as I anticipated. Watch your step, Lucy Hamilton, and get down off your cloud."

Anita glanced at the pastel-colored cover and arched her golden eyebrows slightly. "A pet cemetery? I've heard they are quite the vogue around New York, but didn't realize there was one in Miami."

"We all felt you must be unaware of our existence when we read the newspaper item this morning concerning the departure of your Daffy. We don't ordinarily solicit business, Mrs. Rogell, but we did feel it our duty to offer you an opportunity to avail yourself of our help and our trained personnel."

To Lucy's consternation Anita Rogell shook her head decidedly. "I couldn't do that. I haven't the heart to disturb Daffy now. I'm sure she's comfortable and happy in the spot Charles chose for her final resting place. It would be a desecration to disturb her now."

"I don't see that at all. It's often done . . . you know . . . with human beings. After all, circumstances change. . . ."

"No." Anita closed the booklet and held it out to her. "I do appreciate your coming here and all the information you've given me. I'll be sure to mention *Haven Eternal* to any of my friends who might be interested. But it is too late now to be any help to Daffy."

"Perhaps it isn't, Mrs. Rogell." Lucy Hamilton was thinking fast and extemporizing as she went. "We have a very special service that isn't even mentioned in our regular booklet. It's . . . something we have inaugurated recently for pet owners who feel they will be happier if their loved ones are buried close to them. You definitely must have a marker for Daffy. And we also do individual landscaping of your own private burial plot," she rushed on, "and provide perpetual care if you wish it. Or you can have one of those cunning grottos built right here on your own grounds over the spot where Daffy is already interred."

Anita shook her head firmly. "Not a grotto, I think. It seems ostentatious somehow. A simple granite stone, perhaps, suitably inscribed, of course."

"Of course," breathed Lucy sympathetically.

"And perhaps the grave could be marked with a border of flowers," she added persuasively.

"How much will that be?" asked Anita Rogell.

"We'll have to give you an estimate. Make sketches, you know, and offer you several different plans at various prices. It will run . . . oh, from a minimum of twenty-five dollars up to . . . not more than a hundred I'd say. As soon as I have the physical layout clearly in my mind, I can start our men to work. It would save the cost of a second trip," she urged.

"Yes. I can see that. But I won't be under any obligation to go on with it until I've seen and approved the plans," said Anita a trifle sharply.

"Indeed not. There is no obligation whatsoever." Lucy laughed flutingly. She stood up. "If you can just give me directions so I can find the grave myself . . . ?"

Anita said, "I haven't inquired directly of Charles myself . . . for the exact spot he chose. I was so overwrought last night that I trusted his taste and good judgment." She dropped a languid hand to an ivory-colored telephone handset beside her and pressed a button before lifting the instrument.

Lucy stood back unobtrusively and watched her closely as she spoke into the mouthpiece. It seemed to Lucy her husky voice had a definable lilt to it and the tight serenity of her features relaxed a trifle as she said, "Charles?

Would you please come upstairs?"

She replaced the instrument and said, "My chauffeur will take you to poor Daffy's grave. And I am pleased that you came to talk to me, Miss Hamilton. I think the work you are doing is perfectly wonderful."

A moment later there was a light rap on the door, and Lucy turned to see it open and a stocky young man in dark green uniform with polished leather puttees standing there. He had heavy, clean-shaven features, with piercing black eyes beneath thick brows that met above the bridge of a blunt nose. His chin was square and his lips were full, though somehow they conveyed a hint of cruelty.

His manner was informally respectful without being servile, and his voice was a well-modulated baritone as he said, "What is it, Ma'm?"

"This is Miss Hamilton, Charles." Anita lifted her left hand toward Lucy. "She is from the *Pet Haven Eternal,* and I want you to take her out and show her the spot where Daffy is buried. I may decide to beautify the grave."

He looked at Lucy and nodded gravely without speaking, and stepped back into the hall. Lucy went to the door, saying brightly, "Thank you very much for the time you've given me, Mrs. Rogell. I'm sure you won't be disappointed."

She stepped gladly out of the hot room into the dimly cool hall, and followed the chauffeur who stolidly led her to a narrow rear stairway that led out to the back of the house.

IV

MICHAEL SHAYNE was pacing back and forth between the waiting room and his inner office when Lucy Hamilton returned. He swung on her disappointedly and growled, "I've been waiting for a phone call to come and get the mutt. No soap?"

Lucy shook her head, lifting off her floppy hat and stripping off white gloves. "She wouldn't buy it, Michael. She's positive Daffy will be happier buried right there at home."

"You did see her?"

"Oh, I saw her all right. And gave her the pitch. She just didn't fall for it."

"What's she like, Lucy?"

Lucy Hamilton hesitated and took a deep breath before replying, "Like an angel infested with leprosy, Michael." Her eyes were wide and troubled as they met his searching gaze candidly. "How can I say it? She's devastatingly beautiful . . . with a diseased soul."

Shayne said quietly, "You're trying to say you wouldn't put it past her to murder her husband and then try to murder Henrietta.

if she decided the old gal was a nuisance."

"I guess that is what I'm trying to say. Yet, I have nothing to go on . . . except for her mouth. And that, I'm not going to describe for you. I just hope I'm around the first time you see her."

"Did you manage to see any of the others?"

"A maid named Maybelle who reluctantly let me in. Her charming brother, Marvin Dale . . . and Charles."

Shayne grinned slightly at the change in Lucy's tone when she spoke the chauffeur's name. "Tell me about Charles."

"I got quite well acquainted with Charles in the space of about ten minutes," Lucy said quietly. He's . . . got something, Michael. It's so darned hard to describe . . ." Her voice trailed off as she turned toward the gate in the railing that led to her desk. With her profile to Shayne, she went on slowly, choosing her words carefully, "It's a sort of aura about him. Almost a physical emanation. You feel he's completely primitive. Animal-like." She stopped at the railing and turned a flushed face to him.

"All right," she said fiercely. "I'll say it out loud. He makes a woman feel that loving him would be wild and free and wonderful."

Shayne said quietly, "He must be quite a guy."

"It isn't anything he *does* or says, Michael," she said. "It's the way he *is*. You'll never understand."

"No," said Shayne equably, "I don't suppose I ever will." He lowered one hip to the railing so he was close to Lucy, but he didn't look at her. "You make it sound like a pretty explosive set-up, the way you describe the two of them."

"Oh, I suppose I'm exaggerating horribly. Good heaven! How melodramatic can you get?"

"What about the brother?"

"Marvin? Oh, he's a weak lush."

Shayne tugged at his earlobe. "You make it seem more important than ever to get that dog's stomach contents analyzed. Damn it, Lucy! Do you suppose she suspected what you were after"

"No, I'm sure she didn't." Lucy was composed now, and when Shayne looked at her inquiringly she wrinkled her nose at him and smiled shyly. "I think I've made up my mind," she announced. "I've been arguing with myself about it all the way back from the Rogell estate."

"Made up your mind about *what?*" demanded Shayne.

"Whether I should tell you where Daffy is buried. If I do tell you, I know perfectly well you'll be out there, as soon as it's dark, digging her up. You'll be trespassing and breaking I don't know how many laws . . . and if

Charles should catch you at it . . ." She shuddered and then looked down into her bag with a frown.

Shayne said roughly, "I think I can handle a chauffeur. Do you mean you think he's suspicious?"

Lucy drew a folded sheet of paper from her bag and said composedly, "I wouldn't be at all surprised. It came to me suddenly when Anita absolutely refused to have Daffy dug up and taken to *Haven Eternal*. I made up a wild story about us beautifying graves at home and putting up headstones and even providing individual perpetual care if it was desired. And she fell for it. She called Charles in and told him to show me where Daffy was buried, so I could give her an estimate of the cost. So Charles took me down a rear stairway and out the back and along a path leading to the boathouse."

Lucy paused a moment, studying Shayne's face doubtfully. "It's beautifully landscaped right up to the low bluff overlooking the bay. In back there's a four-car garage with a large apartment above. Charles lives there. The two maids and the housekeeper, Mrs. Blair, have rooms on the third floor of the house," she interpolated. "Charles told me when I asked. And, for no reason at all, he volunteered the information that Mrs. Blair had always had her private suite on the second floor

next to Henrietta until Mr. Rogell married Anita. Then she was moved up with the maids."

Lucy paused a moment, eyes downcast. "That might be important . . . in the light of something Henrietta said this morning. I don't know whether you noticed it or not, Michael, but she started to say something about her brother and Mrs. Blair, and then stopped abruptly."

Shayne said, "I remember. So he led you down this path to the boathouse."

Lucy nodded. "And about a hundred feet from the edge of the bluff, where there are wooden stairs leading down to a private dock and boathouse, there's a huge, old, cypress tree on the right . . . on the left coming from the boathouse." She unfolded her sheet of paper and studied it for a moment.

"I stopped my car as soon as I drove outside, and jotted down some figures. Turning off from the path at right angles to the tree, it's eighteen of my paces to Daffy's grave, before you reach the trunk of the tree, but under the shade. And from the point where you turn off at right angles from the path toward the tree . . . from that point to the top of the stairs is fifty-eight paces. I counted them when I walked down the path pretending I had to get a good view of the bay in order to plan Daffy's landscaping."

Shayne nodded, his face inscrutable. "Is the grave easily distinguishable?"

"It wasn't when he first showed it to me. There's no grass under the tree, and he had smoothed it down so it didn't show very much, but I got him to break off a couple of switches and stick them at each end of the grave so I could find it easily next time I came. I said he might not be around to show me. And that's when I think he started getting a little suspicious. He made a couple of nasty remarks while he was marking it that didn't sound *un*suspicious."

Shayne nodded and drew in a deep breath. "You're terrific, Lucy. It shouldn't be too difficult to judge the distance, even if fifty-eight of your paces would be much shorter than mine. I think I'll try my luck fishing from a rowboat on the bay about dusk tonight. I'll have to manage to locate the Rogell boathouse before dark from out on the bay. That may present a problem." He frowned thoughtfully and glanced at his watch, "Get Tim Rourke on the phone, angel. He's pretty good with a pair of oars."

Lucy compressed her lips and went back to her desk without protesting further. When she had Timothy Rourke on the wire, the readhead said, "Are you very busy, Tim?"

"No more than usual." Alerted by the detective's casual tone, the *Daily News* reporter, added, "Not too busy to get on the trail of a story."

"How'd you like to go fishing?"

After a brief silence, Rourke demanded incredulously, "This *is* Mike Shayne, isn't it? Did you say fishing?"

Shayne grinned at the phone and said, "That's right. You know. in a rowboat on the Bay. With poles and lines with hooks on them."

"What are we going to fish for. Mike?" asked Rourke resignedly.

"A dead dog."

Rourke said, "I see." There was a longer pause this time, then the reporter demanded hopefully. "Have you got in on the Rogell deal?"

"I just suggested going fishing for a dead dog. You want to go along?"

"You bet. When?"

"I think the best time will be shortly after dark, but we should take a boat from the Fisherman's pier a little before sundown. Can you meet me there about seven."

Rourke said, "Will do," and Shayne caught him before he could hang up:

"Know where you can get hold of a shovel?"

"What kind of shovel?"

"One that digs . . . in the ground?"

"I've got a short-handled spade in the back of my car. Look, Mike. If it is the Rogell thing . . ."

Shayne said blandly, "Bring your short-handled spade along, Tim. Fisherman's Wharf at seven. And don't be late."

AT EARLY DUSK that evening a small rowboat was quartering lazily about a half mile offshore on the smooth surface of Biscayne Bay some two miles southwesterly from the municipal docks. Michael Shayne sat in the stern, hunched over with elbows on his knees, wearing a newly-purchased, cheap straw hat, and with a fishing rod extended over the stern trailing a line in the water with an unbaited hook on the end of it.

Timothy Rourke sat toward the bow facing Shayne's hunched back and rowing easily. He had a bottle of bourbon between his feet, and he shipped his oars at brief intervals to take a sip from the bottle.

"I'd guess one of those three boathouses opposite us must be the Rogell place," the redhead said.

"Seems about right," Rourke agreed. "But which one?"

Shayne said, "We can row in closer just as soon as it gets a little darker. Lucy said there was a private dock and stairs leading up the bluff."

Rourke shaded his eyes to study the three boathouses with Shayne, and announced," There's someone just pushing off in a boat from the center dock," he said. "We'd better put on a good fishing act until he's out of sight."

They indulged in no further conversation. Darkness came fast. There was no moon, but the sky was clear and bright starlight glinted on the surface of the bay. Facing toward Shayne in the stern, Rourke kept his eyes fixed on the third-floor lights of the turreted house and kept the boat roughly on course by lifting one hand or the other.

When it nosed alongside the dock, Shayne was leaning out the stern with a mooring line to catch a stanchion, and he made it fast with a double half-hitch. He stepped easily onto the wooden dock and moved forward into the shadow of the boathouse where he turned to see Rourke stepping out with the spade in his hand.

There was utter night-silence about him as he climbed the wooden steps in rubber-soled shoes, and his alert ears caught no sound from Rourke behind him.

At the top, he could glimpse a faint blur of light through shrubbery from the big house some distance beyond, and there was enough starlight to outline the path he was to follow. He strode along it, counting his steps carefully, and stopped on forty-five. On his left, fifty or sixty feet away, silhouetted against the sky, was a towering cypress tree. Shayne walked toward it confidently, again counting his paces. At the count of ten, the blaze of a strong flashlight struck him suddenly in the face

from a point some twenty feet to his right. He stopped in mid-stride as a resonant voice ordered, "Stand still and put your hands in the air."

Shayne stood still and put his hands in the air. Blinking against the glare of the flashlight he could see nothing except the glint of metal at the point of origin of the light. The glint of metal moved and the voice said triumphantly, "Keep your hands high in the air. This is a double-barrelled shotgun with both triggers cocked."

Charles' voice had a note of feline ferocity in it as he said flatly, "And don't try to put on an innocent act. You're that smart private eye, Mike Shayne. I was expecting you after you sent your secretary out to case the layout this afternoon."

"I don't know what you're talking about," Shayne protested. "I'm a tourist from up north and I rented a rowboat . . ." It seemed to him that Charles moved three or four feet closer. That would make it six feet, Shayne calculated. It seemed a satisfactory distance to him.

He tensed as he reached a clump of hibiscus plants close to the house, braced his heels and flung himself backward and down. As he hit the ground full-length with arms still stretched over his head, there was the terrific blast of both barrels of a twelve-gauge directly over his body.

At the same moment his flailing hands fastened on Charles' ankles and he jerked them from under the man and heard the gun fall to the ground. Then Shayne was on his knees furiously driving a left and then a right fist into the whitish blur that was Charles' face as he tried to roll away. His left glanced off the chauffeur's cheekbone, but his right connected solidly with mouth and blunt chin at the precise moment the back of the man's head was in contact with the ground.

There was a splendid crunching sound and Charles' head lolled to the side. Otherwise he did not move.

Shayne dragged himself to his feet and exhaled a great shuddering breath, faintly surprised to find that he was still alive. A bright light sprang on at the back of the house beyond the hibiscus, and in the light Shayne stooped to pick up the shotgun by the end of its twin barrels with his left hand. Then he got a firm grip at the back of Charles neat, green uniform collar, and straightened up and dragged the gun and the unconscious man around the clump shrubbery into the full glare of a floodlight mounted above the kitchen door and directed across the parking space in front of the garage.

Two women stood just outside the open door beneath the floodlight looking at him from a distance of forty feet. One was middle-aged and short and somewhat dumpy, Shayne's first glance told him. The other was young and slender and beautiful. She was bareheaded and dressed all in white, and white draperies trailed out behind her as she sped toward him across the parking space, crying out in a choked voice. "Charles? Is that you?"

Shayne got a grin on his face as he stalked forward dragging Charles and the shotgun behind him. His one fleeting thought was that Lucy was to be deprived of her wish to be on hand the first time he met Anita Rogell.

V

WHEN MRS. ROGELL came close. Shayne relaxed his grip on Charles' collar and the chauffeur slumped forward with his face to the macad-am. Anita dropped to her knees in front of him and crouched there with her hands on his head and cheek, and cried out tearfully, "Charles! Answer me!"

When Charles didn't answer, she looked up fiercely at Shayne and demanded," What have you done to him."

Shayne looked down at the skinned knuckles of his right hand and said, "He'll be all right, Mrs. Rogell. Do you greet all your guests with a double-barreled shot-gun?"

Charles moved his head and groaned thickly. Anita bent over him again, crooning softly, and he twisted his body and got the palms of both hands flat on the pave-ment and hoisted himself up to a half-sitting position. His black eyes were wild and the front of his face was smeared with blood.

He spoke groggily through mashed lips and a hole where two front teeth had been, " 'S Mike Shayne, Nita. I tol' you . . ." He choked on a clot of blood and hacked it out of his throat and then slumped down on his side again.

The older woman had reached the scene and Anita got to her feet, ordering her sharply, "Call Dr. Evans at once, Mrs. Blair. Charles is badly hurt. And tell Martin to come out here if he's sober enough to help. We must get Charles inside."

While the housekeeper scurried away toward the back door, Shayne dropped the shotgun and said, "We don't need any help for that."

He stooped and got his right arm under Charles' thighs, put his left behind his lax shoulders, lift-ed him up, and staggered a step forward, supporting with difficulty the man's heavy bulk.

"Where do you want him?" he ground out through set teeth. "Which way?"

"Here," Anita said, stepping back and gesturing. "Through the back door. You'd never get him up to his apartment over the ga-rage." She hurried in front of him, and Shayne followed, his knees al-most buckling under the strain, but grimly determined to carry it off.

He was halfway across the parking space and was becoming increasingly aware that he couldn't possibly make it, when Charles fortuitously gurgled something deep in his throat and began mak-ing feeble efforts to free himself from Shayne's arms.

The redhead thankfully low-ered his right arm to let the chauf-feur's dangling feet touch the ground, and got Charles' left arm around his neck where he levered it down over his own left shoulder. The man was conscious enough to support part of his weight on rub-bery legs, and Shayne half-carried him on to the back door where Anita was waiting.

"In here." She went through a gleaming modern kitchen to a small room directly off it fitted up as a comfortable sitting room. The housekeeper was talking excitedly into a telephone in one corner, and Shayne thankfully let Charles down on a chintz-covered sofa where he lay very still, glaring up at Shayne balefully.

Mrs. Blair replaced the phone and bustled forward, saying cheerfully, "Dr. Evans will be right here. Now you just lie easy, Charles, and I'll get a cold cloth for that face of yours."

She hurried through the connecting door into the kitchen and Shayne slowly turned his gaze away from Charles' venomous glare to catch a queer look on Anita's face as she stood back and to one side, studying him and not paying the slightest heed to the chauffeur.

When she spoke her voice was throaty and had a little catch in it. "You're Michael Shayne."

He said, "I'm Michael Shayne. Does that give your man license to hunt me down like a mad dog with a shotgun?"

From the sofa, Charles uttered garbled words. Neither of them paid him the slightest heed. They were warily measuring each other like antagonists in a duel to the death.

She sucked in her breath and said, "He warned me you would come tonight. To try and dig Daffy up and take her away."

Shayne said heatedly, "I don't know what you're talking about. I explained to your chauffeur that I got lost in the dark while fishing, and rowed in to the first shore lights I saw . . . hoping I could call a taxi to take me home. And he met me with a cocked shotgun."

"Why did you send your secretary here this afternoon . . . if not to discover where Daffy is buried so you could come and take her away?"

"My secretary?" said Shayne in feigned astonishment. "Are all of you crazy?"

"She is named Lucy Hamilton, isn't she?"

"That's my secretary's name," Shayne admitted. "As a great many people in Miami know. What of it?"

"Do you deny she came here this afternoon pretending to be from a pet cemetery so she could find where Daffy is buried?"

"Of course, I deny it," said Shayne vehemently. "Why on earth would Lucy do a silly thing like that?"

"Because Charles suspects that John's crazy sister hired you to try and prove Daffy was poisoned by one of us here because she accused us of murdering her brother." Anita spoke the words calmly and simply, as though they were of no consequence at all.

Shayne drew in a deep breath

and shook his red head in what he hoped was a gesture of utter bafflement.

"You're 'way beyond me. I don't follow you at all."

"I did call *Haven Eternal* after Charles came back from showing Miss Hamilton Daffy's grave and told me he thought she was up to something else. They have no representative named Lucy Hamilton, and they don't even send out people representing them. How do you explain that, Michael Shayne?"

Shayne said, "I don't. Why should I?"

Anita tilted her head and considered him gravely for a moment. Then with a startlingly sudden change of mood she put out her hand and Shayne took it in his and she said almost gaily, "I've a feeling you'd like a drink, Michael Shayne, and have been too stubbornly angry to ask me." Her husky voice made rich music of the name.

With her hand in his, she led him past the sofa where Mrs. Blair was on her knees still making clucking noises over Charles. They went out of the room and through the kitchen to the wide, vaulted hallway that Lucy had described to Shayne, and some thirty feet down the hall toward the front door and through a pair of sliding doors on the right that stood partially open. It was a small conservatory, and the temperature inside was the same as Lucy had described as existing in the upstairs boudoir.

She said, "Marvin and I had stingers after dinner. Would you like to mix another batch?"

Shayne squeezed her hand hard, hoping she wouldn't think his switch to a sudden warmth too abrupt, and looked down at the top of her shining head which lightly brushed his shoulder. He released her hand and said, "I'd rather have a straight drink." He reached for one of the cocktail glasses.

Anita moved toward a silken bell-cord, murmuring, "I'll ring for a clean glass."

Shayne said, "Please don't. I'd much rather use one of these and be alone here with you." He twisted the glass stopper from the large decanter and filled one of the cocktail glasses to the brim.

She had moved back close to him when he lifted it to his lips. He breathed in deeply the clean, delightful bouquet from the distillate of sun-ripened grapes, and the tips of her taut, full breasts, behind the silky white of a loose blouse, pressed lightly against his chest as she moved even closer.

She stood rigid, just touching him, her arms straight down at her sides and both hands tightly clenched. Over the rim of his glass, he stared down into her invitingly amorous eyes.

It was either a brief moment or an eternity that they stood like hat, as close as two humans can get. Then Shayne heard the insistent ringing of door chimes from the front, and he slowly released her and stepped back to pick up the cocktail glass in a trembling hand, just as Mrs. Blair hurried past the open doors on her way to answer the front door.

Anita smiled dreamily at him and rested the knuckles of her left hand on top of the table. "I imagine that will be Dr. Evans come to see Charles. He's always so prompt."

Shayne took a gulp of cognac. It burned all the way down his throat to meet but not assuage another sort of burning in the pit of his stomach. He said, "That's nice of Dr. Evans," set his glass down and fumbled a cigarette out of his shirt pocket while Anita sauntered to the gap in the sliding doors and stood there looking out composedly until Mrs. Blair and the doctor hurried by.

"Let me know about Charles at once, Doctor," she said. "I do hope it isn't serious." She turned back to Shayne and said serenely, "I'm sure Charles was exactly right and Henrietta did hire you to dig up Daffy and try and prove she was poisoned."

"Was she?" demanded Shayne.

"Poisoned? Of course not. Why would anyone want to do a cruel thing like that? Everyone loved her. Except Henrietta, of course. She hated everyone. If Daffy was poisoned, you can be sure that old hag did it. And maybe she did at that," Anita went on slowly. "It'd be just like her. She could have, you know. Poisoned that chicken herself, and then fed a plate of it to dear Daffy out of spite."

Shayne grinned sardonically. "And then went around and hired a private detective to disinter the dog and prove her guilt? You can't have it both ways, Anita."

"Maybe not, but you can be certain no one else in this household would have harmed Daffy."

"How can you be so certain of that?" sneered a rather fruity voice from the hallway, and a fair-haired young man lolled between the parted doors. He swayed a little and clenched a highball glass in his hand, and his bloodshot eyes didn't focus very well.

"This is Michael Shayne," said Anita distinctly. "My brother, Marvin."

"The famous private eye, eh?" Marvin blinked at him and moved closer to peer into his face with bleared eyes. "You don't look the part at all, you know. Not like it is on television with all your beautiful blonde clients ripping off their clothes and crawling into bed with you first crack out of the box. Does he, Sis?"

In a coldly vicious voice, Anita said, "Get out of here, Marvin. You're drunk."

"Coursh I'm a little bit drunkie." He smiled vacuously and took one more look at Shayne, shuddered and almost fell over his own feet exiting.

She said, "So much for my brother, Mr. Shayne." A dreamily contemplative expression chased the anger from her face. "I would, you know. Just like all those blondes he was talking about."

Shayne said, "I know," very matter-of-factly.

She closed her eyes and clasped her arms about her full breasts and shivered. Then she started gliding toward him with her eyes closed.

Shayne emptied his glass and set it on the table and waited for her to reach him.

The voices of Mrs. Blair and Dr. Evans came from the hall, approaching them. Anita stopped three feet from Shayne, unclasped her arms and opened her eyes. The hypnotized expression faded from her face, and she turned and went to the door and asked lightly, "How is Charles, Doctor?"

"As well as can be expected." His enunciation was precise, with a studiedly genteel inflection. "I had to take six stitches and administer a sedative for the pain. Later, he'll have to see a good dentist. I must have the straight of this, Anita. From Charles and Mrs. Blair I am given to understand that some hulking brute of a private detective forced his way onto your property tonight bent on desecrating the grave of your dog, and Charles was injured while defending the

place. Have you called the police to lay charges against this ruffian? I am required to report the incident, you know."

"Why don't you discuss it with Mr. Shayne?" Anita moved aside and Dr. Albert Evans stepped through the sliding doors. He was young for a practicing M.D. Not more than his early thirties, Shayne thought. He was slender and of medium-height, with slightly protuberant eyes behind gold-rimmed nose glasses attached to a black cord around his neck.

He stopped and looked severely at Shayne, but the detective could have sworn there was the suggestion of a twinkle in his eyes as he asked, "What did you hit Charles with? He insists you attacked him with a large rock."

Shayne held out his right hand with the fist doubled. "If you've any adhesive left you might put a little on my knuckles."

The doctor took off his glasses, blinked rapidly and fiddled with them. "I've done all I can for Charles tonight." He turned to go, but Shayne stopped him.

"If you're going toward town, Doctor, could I bum a ride with you? I meant to call a cab, but haven't gotten around to it yet."

"Why yes. Certainly, if you like. I go down the Avenue to Flagler."

"Right past my place," Shayne told him genially. He walked past Anita and her fingers swung out to catch his hand as he went by. He pressed her fingertips hard and said, "Thanks for everything, Mrs. Rogell. I hope we meet again."

She dug her fingernails fiercely into the fleshy part of his palm and then released his hand. He followed Dr. Evans down the hall, glancing through *portières* on the left as he went by and seeing Marvin across the library at the bar intent on mixing himself another drink.

Five minutes later Shayne, sitting at ease in Dr. Evans' car, with the house three miles behind them, said in an even voice, "You think the dog was poisoned?"

Evans glanced sideways at him. "I have no opinion in the matter . . . not being a veterinarian. I do wish Mrs. Rogell had not been so precipitate in having the little beast buried. But she has a dreadful complex about death in any form. The result of some childhood trauma, I daresay, though I'm not a psychiatrist either. And the death of her husband, just two days ago, left her dreadfully upset, of course. A remarkable woman, though. She's bearing up exceedingly well."

"I understand you signed the death certificate," Shayne said.

"Certainly, I did. I had been attending him for months and was called immediately after his death was discovered."

"Is there any possibility whatsoever, Doctor, that he could have been poisoned?"

"You've been listening to Henrietta," he said bitterly. "Spreading her spleen wherever anyone will listen. Mr. Shayne, if you are an experienced detective, you must know that no competent medical man in his right mind can absolutely rule out the possibility of some kind of poison in *any* death. No matter how normal it may appear on the surface. If we took that fact into consideration, perhaps we should have an autopsy on every cadaver . . . no matter what the circumstances of death."

"Perhaps we should," Shayne said equably.

"Yes . . . well . . ." The doctor slowed as he approached the bridge across the Miami River. "Since that is not accepted practice, I can only tell you there was no scintilla of evidence to give me the slightest doubt that John Rogell's death was the normal and natural result of his heart condition. That is the statement I gave the police, and I stand behind it."

"Right here, Doctor," Shayne said hastily as they drew abreast of his apartment hotel. "Thanks for the lift . . . and for the information."

He got out at curb and lifted a big hand in farewell, waited until the doctor drove on and then trudged across to the side entrance where he climbed one flight of stairs and went to his corner apartment to wait for Timothy Rourke to show up or telephone him.

VI

IT WAS ALMOST two hours and three drinks later when the door opened and Timothy Rourke shambled inside with his trench-coat belted tightly about his thin waist.

He said, "By God, Mike! You're one who'd come up dressed for the opera if you fell into the charcoal pit at a clambake."

Shayne grinned amiably and asked, "Had rough going?"

"Look at my goddamned hands." Rourke strode forward, holding the palms up for Shayne's inspection. They were puffed with blisters, some of which had broken and the red flesh beneath was cracked and bleeding. "Been rowing around in circles on that lousy bay for two hours," grated Rourke. "These blisters will last a week."

He turned aside to a wall liquor cabinet and lifted down a bottle of straight bourbon with the ease of long familiarity. He pulled the cork as he returned to the center table, tilted the bottle over a tumbler containing two half-melted ice cubes and a small quantity of water that Shayne had been using for a chaser. He poured four fingers into the glass, sloshed it about for a moment, and then drank it off in four gulps.

He smacked his lips expressively, draped his knobby body into a chair across the table and grated, "The things I do for you, Mike Shayne! By God, that dog had better have poison in her belly."

"She has," Shayne said flatly.

"You got her, huh?"

"Sure I got her," said Rourke belligerently. "While you were inside getting cozy with the widow. I got a peek through the bushes after the shotgun blasted. I figured I'd take one look at you with your fool head blown off so I could give Lucy the morbid details, And what did I see? You standing there under the floodlight with that unconscious lug in your arms, and that babe fawning up at you like she'd never seen a man before in her life."

"Where's the dog?" Shayne asked abruptly.

"Downstairs in my car." Rourke sighed and pulled himself to his feet with a grimace of pain from long unused muscles. He went out to the kitchen to get a fresh glass and more ice cubes for himself while Shayne found the number of Miami's most noted toxicologist, lifted the phone and gave it to the switchboard downstairs.

Shayne spoke into the mouthpiece as Rourke sauntered back and sloshed whiskey into the glass: "Is that Bud Tolliver? Mike Shayne, Bud. Can you do a fast job for me tonight?"

He listened a moment and said, "I don't think this will take long. You should be able to handle it right there in your basement lab. Analysis of the stomach contents of a dead dog for poison. I'll bring it right over to your place." He hung up and told Rourke, "Tolliver feels his professional status is being impugned by working on a dog. Coming along, Tim?"

Rourke had sunk back into his chair with tall glass clamped tightly in both hands. He shook his head, got a leather key-case from his pocket and dropped it on the table. "Take my car. It's parked in front with the dog locked in the luggage compartment. Drop Daffy off at Bud's and then come here, huh? I'm trying to remember something about Henrietta Rogell. If it comes through, I think we can stand a trip to the *News* morgue. If it doesn't, at least I'll be catching up with you." He lifted his glass significantly.

Shayne took the keys and said, "Try to make it come through, Tim."

He went out the door and down on the elevator, through a deserted lobby to Rourke's battered sedan in front.

Bud Tolliver was a bachelor who lived in a five-room stucco house in the northeast section of the city. The porch light was on when Shayne pulled up in front of the house, and the redhead got out and unlocked the luggage compartment and opened it. The tiny body of a Pekinese lay stiff-legged on the floor, its formerly shiny coat matted with dirt, its mouth half open

in what appeared to be a derisive grin.

Shayne lifted the light body out by a front and rear paw, carried it up the walk held stifly out in front of him, and the front door opened as he stepped onto the porch, and Tolliver motioned him inside.

The toxicologist was as tall as Shayne, and a few years younger. His head was completely bald, and he had an intelligent, bony face that puckered thoughtfully as he drew aside and looked at the detective's burden. "How long has the pooch been buried?"

"She's supposed to have died last evening in convulsions about ten minutes after eating a dish of creamed chicken fed to her by an old lady who suspected it contained poison. On the other hand it's reported that she's been a sickly dog, often subject to stomach upsets."

"The convulsions in ten minutes sounds like a solid dose of strychnine," said Tolliver absently, lifting a starched surgeon's garment from a hook on the wall and sliding his arms into the sleeves. "If so, it'll be easy."

"It needs to be definitely tied in with the creamed chicken to give us an open and shut case, Bud."

"Sure," the toxicologist said cheerfully. "I'll do my best. You want to stick around and watch it done?"

"I don't think so," said Shayne hastily. "Not tonight. Tim Rourke and I have things to do. Call me at home, huh? About how long?"

"Half an hour or so."

Shayne said, "Swell," and went up the stairs quickly while Tolliver bent over the dead dog with professional interest and zeal.

Timothy Rourke got to his feet quickly when Shayne walked into his own apartment ten minutes later. He drained the last of his drink and said triumphantly, "Got it, Mike. Let's run up to the *News* and check it out."

Shayne waited at the door for him to come out, and pulled it shut on the latch, and asked, "Got what?" as they went back to the elevator.

"The thing that's been nibbling at my so-called memory ever since you sprung this Rogell deal on me this afternoon. Gives a pretty good sidelight on Henrietta. It was about five years ago, Mike, when she made the headlines with a lawsuit against her brother. Demanding an accounting of his estate and claiming a one-half share for herself.

"The details are hazy in my mind," he went on as they crossed the lobby. "I forget how it came out. But he made his fortune out west, in mining, I think, and I believe that she claimed she worked in the mines with him and that half his millions were rightfully hers, and she wanted the money legally and in her own name instead of living with him in that big house and having him dole it out to her."

A half hour later in the huge file room in the *Daily News* Tower, Rourke led the way confidently down a long aisle lined with filing cabinets, pulling dangling cords to switch on overhead lights as he went. He slowed and finally stopped in front of a cabinet, pulled out a drawer marked Re-Ro, and slowly turned clippings over as he spoke.

"Here's the old boy's wedding just a few months ago. The April-December wedding that had the sob-sisters gushing all over the society pages."

Shayne leaned over to study the picture with him. It had been taken on the steps of a local church as the bridal couple left after the ceremony. It was the first picture Shayne remembered seeing of John Rogell. He was tall and lean and leathery-faced like his sister, wearing top hat and cutaway. He looked a sound and vigorous sixty in the picture, not like a doddering old man whose heart might be expected to give way under the importunities of a demanding young bride.

Of course, there was a startling difference between the ages of the couple. In her white bridal dress and clutching her wedding bouquet, Anita was radiantly beautiful, the personification of a virginal young bride on the happiest day of her life.

"Mr. and Mrs. John Rogell as they emerged from the noonday solemnizing of their wedding rites," Rourke read drily from the text beneath the picture. "Hell, if the old boy had three months of that, I'd guess he died happy."

He turned the clippings back slowly. "There were scads of feature stories as soon as news of the engagement broke. It was real Cinderella stuff. It *can* and *does* happen in Miami. Anita Dale. Small-town girl, from a poor upstate family, coming timidly to seek her fortune in the Magic City of sun, sin and sex. Six months later she sits out in that stone mansion heir to a lot of millions of bucks. How's that for rags-to-riches in one easy installment?"

"Did you say she worked in the Peabody Brokerage firm?"

"Sure. Harold Peabody. She was working there as a filing clerk when she met Rogell. Peabody is one of Miami's up-and-coming young financial consultants. Rogell is probably his biggest account, though others have been flocking to him since he got publicity along with one of his secretaries marrying millions. It's pretty well understood he'll be executor of Rogell's estate. But that's all recent history," Rourke added as he flipped back through scattered clippings. "Just routine stuff here. Rogell buys another shipping line, invests a million in an Atlanta real estate

development. Here's what I'm looking for."

He paused at a long front-page story, head-lined, "SPINSTER SUES MULTI-MILLIONAIRE BROTHER."

"This is the day they opened the trial," he muttered. "I covered that first day myself. Let's see . . . if I turn back a few clippings we should find the verdict."

He began doing so, glancing quickly and expertly at a few words or the heading of each story. He stopped after a moment and said, "Here it is," and read: JURY RETURNS VERDICT IN MILLION-DOLLAR SUIT FOR DEFENDANT."

"She lost it hands-down," he told Shayne. "I thought I remembered it that way, but I wasn't sure. The jury felt Henrietta was doing all right as she was . . . sharing the big house with him as his official hostess with charge accounts all over town and a monthly cash allowance a lot bigger than she could possibly spend."

Shayne said, "Turn back two or three of those clippings, Tim. During the progress of the trial. There was one story I noticed as you slid by looking for the verdict."

"Which one?" Rourke turned one clipping after another to face up to the light.

Shayne said, "There it is." It was a two-column inside-page story, headed "HOUSEKEEPER TESTIFIES," and beneath it there was a somewhat blurred cut of a rather pretty and slightly plump young woman standing on the front porch of a weathered frame house with a crudely painted sign over her head that said "BLAIR'S BOARDING HOUSE". The caption read: *"Betty Blair in front of her boarding house in Central City, Colorado."* The other picture showed the same woman some thirty years older, still smooth-faced and comely, but some twenty pounds heavier, and was captioned: *"Mrs. Blair as she appeared in court today."*

Rourke nodded and said, "I was in court that day. Henrietta's attorneys called the Rogell housekeeper to testify for the plaintiff, but she was practically a hostile witness and didn't help the case much. Seems she ran a boarding house in the mining town where Rogell started his fortune, and she did testify somewhat reluctantly that people in the town still told stories about how Henrietta actually shouldered a pick in the old days right beside her brother in their first prospect tunnel. Seems they both boarded at her place in later days, and, after Mr. Blair died, John Rogell went out to Colorado and brought her back here and installed her as his housekeeper.

"There were a few attempts by the defense attorney to insinuate that she might have been something more than just his housekeeper, but the judge quashed those fast, ruling that he was incriminating his own witness. In the long run, the Blair testimony helped Rogell, because she was emphatic that he never denied Henrietta anything, never questioned how much money she spent or for what.

"There were three women on the jury," Rourke ended with a chuckle, "and you could see them drooling and wishing they were in Henrietta's shoes."

Shayne nodded and straightened up and glanced at his watch. "Tolliver has had the dog more than half an hour. Let's get back and see if there's any word."

His telephone was ringing when he unlocked the door of his apartment. He hurried to it without turning on a light, snatched it up and barked, "Hello."

Tolliver's voice answered him. "Got it, Mike."

"Got what?"

"Enough strychnine to kill a large family in that creamed chicken the Peke ate."

Shayne said exultantly, "Will Gentry will want this straight from the horse's mouth, Bud. Stay by the phone and I'll have him call you."

The detective gave Gentry's home telephone number to the switchboard, and told Rourke while he waited, "You got those blisters in a good cause. Strychnine. Now we'll move."

Chief of Police Will Gentry's gruff voice came sleepily over the wire, and Shayne told him, Bud

Tolliver's got news for you, Will. About a dead dog."

"The Rogell pooch?" Gentry's voice came awake fast. "By God, Mike, I didn't think you could pull it off. What's the verdict?"

"Ask Tolliver. He's waiting for your call." Shayne gave Gentry the number. "Call me back, huh?"

"Right."

Shayne hung up and said happily, "This calls for a small libation." He poured a drink of Hennessy and waited until Rourke had put whiskey in his glass. He said solemnly, "To the best graverobber I know," and drank his off while Rourke bowed with mock humility before following suit.

His phone rang again and Will Gentry said, "Congratulations, Mike. I'm ordering an immediate P.M. on Rogell. Thank God he's slated to be cremated, so the body hasn't been embalmed."

"Can you do it without a court order or getting permission from the family?"

"With this sort of evidence, yes."

Shayne hung up and looked at his watch, his rugged face tensely alert. He muttered to Rourke, "I better call Lucy. She'll have her fingernails chewed down to the quick by this time." He lifted the phone again and gave her number.

He sat and listened to the telephone ring in her apartment, the alertness slowly fading from his face to be replaced by a disbe-lieving frown. After the tenth ring, he broke the connection.

"She's at home," said Shayne fiercely. "I know how Lucy is. She knew we were making a try for the dog tonight, and she *knew* I'd phone her the first moment . . ."

He broke off as the ringing stopped and the operator asked, "Want I should keep on trying, Mr. Shayne? That's fifteen rings and she still don't answer."

Shayne said, "No," and hung up. There were deep trenches in his cheeks and his eyes were bleak as he hung up and reached for his drink.

"Well, hell," said Rourke reasonably. "A gal can't be expected to sit at home alone by the telephone every night in the week just because her boss is on a case. She knows you can take care of yourself."

Shayne said, "Sure." He drained his glass and set it down slowly.

Rourke studied his friend's trenched face for a moment, cocking his head on one side and narrowing his eyes. "She didn't *say* she was going to sit at home and wait for a call, did she?"

Shayne said, "No," through clenched teeth.

The telephone started ringing then. Shayne turned back to the table and grabbed it fast. It was the clerk downstairs.

"There's a Western Union messenger here, Mr. Shayne. Shall I send him up?"

Shayne said, "Yes," and exhaled a deep sigh as he dropped the receiver. He told Rourke happily, "A telegram. Lucy must have had to go out for something and knew I'd be worried."

A moment later the elevator door clanged open down the hall and they heard footsteps approaching the door.

Shayne went to the door, and pulled it open. A wizened little man stood in the doorway wearing an oversized messenger's uniform. He intoned, "Message for Mr. Michael Shayne," and deftly exchanged a white envelope for the coin in Shayne's hand.

Shayne's expression changed as he looked down at the envelope, with his name and address penciled in crude print on the outside. He exclaimed, "Wait a minute. This isn't a telegram."

The messenger said placidly, "It sure ain't. But it's for you if you're him that's writ down there." He started to turn away, but the detective grated, "Wait a minute," as he tore the envelope open. There was a single folded sheet torn from a yellow scratchpad inside. In the same crude printing as the address, Shayne read:

You got the dog but we got your secretary. If you want to see her alive again, throw the pooch in the bay and forget you ever saw her.

The message was unsigned.

Shayne grabbed the messenger's thin arm and demanded harshly, "Where did you get this?"

"Corner of Miami Avenue and Fourth. Shamrock Bar."

"Who gave it to you to bring here?"

"Bartender had it for me." The messenger twisted uneasily, dropping his rheumy gaze from Shayne's hot eyes. "Paid me two bucks and said to deliver it right away."

Shayne's face was flushed.

"How did you know to go there and pick it up?"

"Central office sent me. We get calls like that all the time. Pick-up and deliver."

Shayne let go his arm and he scuttled down the hall toward the elevator.

VII

"WHAT IS IT, Mike?" Rourke was beside him, his voice anxious. Shayne didn't reply, merely handed Rourke the sheet of yellow paper. He whirled around and strode to the center table, opened the telephone book and riffled through the pages to the Rogell number. He gave it to the operator and waited for a long time with the receiver to his ear. A woman's voice finally said, "Mrs. Rogell's residence."

"This is the police," said Shayne curtly. "Sergeant Hanson speaking. I want to talk to the Rogell chauffeur at once."

"Charles?" He was certain it was Mrs. Blair's voice. "I'm afraid that's impossible. He's sleeping now . . . under heavy sedation."

"Is Mrs. Rogell's brother still there?"

"Marvin's here, all right, but you won't get much out of him either. He didn't need any pills to pass out cold."

Shayne hung up the receiver, shaking his head at Rourke. "No help there. The housekeeper claims both Charles and the brother are dead to the world and can't be awakened."

"I been thinking, Mike. Whoever snatched Lucy and wrote this note thinks you got it before you had time to do anything with the dog. They wouldn't know about Tolliver doing a fast job for you. If you can keep them thinking that . . ."

Shayne said, "Yeh." He lifted the phone again and gave Will Gentry's home telephone number. When the chief answered, he said, "Mike Shayne again, Will. Something has come up at this end." The urgency in his voice kept Gentry from asking any questions. "Have you ordered the autopsy?"

"Sure. They should have already picked the body up from the undertaker's."

"How many people know that?"

"Nobody outside the department except the undertaker, and he's sworn to secrecy. Doc Higgins

promised him he'd have the corpse back in its casket tomorrow morning so no one will know."

Shayne breathed a fervent, "Thank God," and then went on strongly, "Promise me this, Will. Don't take any action tomorrow no matter what the P.M. says. Not till you talk to me first. Will you promise that?"

"Now, wait a minute, Mike. What gives?"

Shayne hesitated, then said flatly, "They've got Lucy. She'll stay alive as long as they think we haven't found poison inside the dog and haven't autopsied Rogell. If he can be cremated tomorrow with them still thinking that . . ."

"Lucy?" rumbled Gentry. "Who's they?"

"That's what I've got to have time to find out, Will. Someone who doesn't want an autopsy on Rogell. So, for the love of God, keep it quiet, Will."

Gentry said gruffly, "I like Lucy, too. You want help?"

"That's what I don't want right now. Just complete secrecy on the autopsy . . . and a call as soon as you know."

Gentry said, "You'll have that," and Shayne hung up.

He got up and said, "Drive me out to Lucy's, Tim. Maybe we can pick something up there."

Downstairs, Shayne stopped at the desk to tell the clerk, "I'll be at Miss Hamilton's number in about fifteen minutes. Try her phone if anything comes up."

He got in the driver's seat of Rourke's car and headed toward Miami Avenue, explaining, "We'll stop at the Shamrock first."

"I don't get this, Mike. How could anyone get to Lucy so fast? None of the people involved know her, do they?"

"She was out there this afternoon. Charles was smart enough to figure she was my secretary, and the rest of them knew what he suspected."

"But she's not listed in the phone book. This may all be a bluff."

Shayne said, "Maybe." He was driving north on Miami Avenue, and slowed as he approached Fourth Street. A corner saloon had a sign in green neon, SHAMROCK BAR. He parked and they got out.

It was a small bar, dingy and dimly-lighted. At this hour there were only three men on stools with drinks in front of them. The bartender was thin and sallow-faced, wearing a dirty white jacket. He came toward them incuriously as they ranged up against the front end of the bar.

Shayne got out his wallet and extracted a ten-dollar bill, smoothed it flat on the bar between his big hands. He moved the bill forward and said," We're not ordering. I just want to ask you a question."

The bartender put his fingertips on the bill but did not pick it up.

His pale blue eyes studied Shayne's face warily. "Sure, Mister. Go ahead and ask."

"A messenger from Western Union picked up an envelope from you fifteen or twenty minutes ago. Tell me about it."

"What about it?"

"Everything."

The man shrugged, keeping the tips of his fingers on the bill, but not drawing it toward him. "There was this guy came in and busted a ten for a boiler-maker and asked could he use the phone. I said sure." The bartender jerked his head to a coin telephone on the wall behind him. "I was standing close enough to hear him ask for Western Union, and then say to send a messenger to make a pick-up from here for immediate delivery. Then he asked what the charge would be for downtown Miami, and then hung up.

"He came back to his drink, and gave me these two envelopes, see? And three ones. Said he was in a hurry and would I give the letters and the money to the messenger when he came. I said sure, and that's all there was to it."

Shayne said hoarsely, "Two envelopes?"

"Yeh. There was two. Just alike. Addressed with a pencil."

"Addressed to whom?" Shayne's voice was unnecessarily harsh.

The bartender looked at him with a touch of belligerence. "How do I know, Mister? None of my business and I didn't pry. I just laid them on the cash register with the three bills, and gave 'em to the messenger when he came. Anything wrong in that?"

Shayne slowly exhaled a long-held breath. He said, "No. Nothing wrong with that. You're sure you didn't see either of the names? It would be worth twice that bill to me."

"Gee, I wisht I had." The bartender sounded truly sorry that he hadn't been more curious. "I just didn't look."

"What did the man look like?"

"Like a bum," he said promptly. "Wearing a ragged coat and needing a haircut. Thin and hungry looking. Hell, I didn't pay heed. Twenty-five or maybey thirty. Just a medium-looking bum."

"But you'd know him if he ever comes in again?" persisted Shayne.

The bartender screwed up his blue eyes. "I . . . reckon I might."

"If he does show his face there'll be ten bills like that in it for you, if you call the police and hold him till they get here."

"Well, sure," said the man uncomfortably. "If the law wants him . . ."

Shayne said emphatically, "They do," and finished his drink.

As they got back into his car, Timothy Rourke said worriedly, "I guess that didn't help much."

"Not a damned bit. Whoever sent the note covered his tracks perfectly. Some hobo off a park bench who was delighted to earn the rest of a ten-dollar bill by having a drink in a bar and calling Western Union."

"The *notes*," Rourke reminded him emphatically as he swung around the corner and headed east on Fourth. "Who was the other one to?"

Shayne shrugged. "For you, maybe. If anyone knew you were with me tonight and it was you who did the actual grave-robbing."

"No one knew that. I swear no one saw me there."

"Lucy knew you were going with me," Shayne reminded him, and neither one of them said any more until Shayne unlocked Lucy's first-floor apartment, east of Biscayne Boulevard with a key that Lucy had given him many years before and which he had never used until tonight.

In a completely calm and exceedingly quiet voice which revealed to his old friend the intensity of the emotion he felt, Shayne said, "You stay here in the sitting room, Tim. I want to go through the place alone. There may be something out of place . . . something I'll recognize."

Awkwardly, Timothy Rourke said, "Sure, Mike. You go right ahead." He leaned against the doorframe, digging out a cigarette and lighting it while he watched Shayne's tall frame move slowly away from him with shoulders squared and chin thrust out.

The detective noted three cigarette butts in the glass ashtray on the coffee table near the end where Lucy generally sat when they were in the apartment together. That meant a couple hours of occupancy to Shayne, indicating she had come in after a leisurely dinner and relaxed for a couple of hours before going out again. There was a single dried ring on the glass table beside the ashtray. Lucy's ingrained tidiness would never have left that ring undisturbed had she finished her drink and gone off to bed without interruption.

Rourke was still standing beside the door when he reentered the sitting room. Shayne's face was somber.

Rourke said, "What do you make of it?"

"Not much this far. Lucy was here . . . alone . . . for a couple of hours after dinner. Had one drink and left in a hurry."

"Under duress?"

Shayne shrugged. "I should guess not. There'd be an overturned glass . . . something to signal me. She'd know I'd be around . . ."

His voice trailed off. He moved to the telephone and stared down moodily at the clean white pad beside it. No telephone numbers jotted, not even a doodle. But Lucy was not the doodling kind, he reminded himself.

He went into the neat bedroom in which the only sign of disarray or hurried departure was a pair of furry mules lying on their sides near the foot of the bed. With his intimate knowledge of Lucy's habits, Shayne knew she had changed to them immediately after coming in, had hurriedly kicked them off and put on her shoes before going out again. It was another sign of hurried departure, but not necessarily of coercion.

"I don't think she had any idea what she was getting into, Tim," he said. "She'd have managed to do *something* . . . leave *some* sort of sign for me . . ."

Lucy Hamilton's telephone rang.

Shayne's shoulders jerked. He crossed to the instrument in two strides and said, "Hello," into the mouthpiece.

The voice that answered him was deep and strong, but undoubtedly feminine. "Is that you, Mr. Shayne?"

"Yes."

"Your hotel gave me this number. Henrietta Rogell."

Again, Shayne said, "Yes?"

"I must see you at once. At the Waldorf Towers. It's a matter I cannot discuss over the telephone."

Her voice was inflexibly determined, and Shayne wasted no time in what he realized would be useless argument. He said, "In a few minutes, Miss Rogell," dropped the receiver and strode toward Rourke who was already on his feet draining his glass.

Without pausing on his way to the door, he said, "The Waldorf Towers, Tim. Drop me there and I'll pick up my car at the dock later."

VIII

HENRIETTA MET him at the door of her suite wearing a faded gray bathrobe, cut along mannish lines, tightly belted about her lean waist, and with comfortable-looking carpet slippers on her bare feet. Her grayish hair was released from its tight bun, tied behind her head with a black ribbon in a sort of pony-tail and fluffed out loosely about her face to soften the hardness of her features somewhat.

She drew him quickly into the sitting room of the pleasantly-decorated suite, shut the door without preamble and took a folded sheet of yellow paper from a pocket of her bathrobe and handed it to him. "This was delivered at the desk half an hour ago," she said, her voice shaking with the intensity of her emotion. By a Western Union messenger, they said."

Shayne read the same penciled writing as his own message:

The dog is already dead but Lucy Hamilton ain't—yet. Tell Shayne we mean business.

Henrietta sat on one end of the sofa and watched the redhead's face while he read it. "What does it mean?" she demanded. "Isn't Lucy Hamilton the name of your secretary—the girl I met in your office."

Shayne nodded. He got out his message and handed it to her. "Both these were given to a downtown bartender about an hour ago by a derelict for delivery to us."

She read his note. "Then you did get hold of the dog?" There was a glitter of excitement in her eyes. "As soon as you find she died from eating my poisoned creamed chicken, you can get an order delaying the funeral until they can do an autopsy on John, can't you?"

Shayne said, "If the dog *was* poisoned. If I go on and have her stomach contents analyzed."

"*If* you do," she said sharply. "Isn't that what I hired you for?"

Shayne sat down in a deep chair in front of her and crossed his long legs. He tugged at his left earlobe and said, "You've read those two notes. I was in Lucy Hamilton's apartment when you phoned, and she's missing. I think I'm going to step out of this case, Miss Rogell. My hands are tied as long as they've got Lucy."

"You can't. I won't have it. I demand possession of that dog's body. I paid for it."

Shayne shook his head. "I'll return your check tomorrow."

"I'll refuse to accept it. I'll sue you. Now you listen to me, young man . . ."

"You listen to me." He didn't raise his voice but there was a finality about his tone that checked her protest. "Your brother is dead. Lucy Hamilton is alive. I want her to stay alive. It's that simple."

"So you'll kow-tow to them? Let them get away with murder just because . . ."

"Just because I may save my secretary's life by so doing." Shayne's voice was harsh. "Exactly. Now that you understand the situation, you can cooperate by telling me anything that might help get her back. Once she's safe, I'm perfectly willing to go ahead . . . but not before."

"But the funeral is at noon. John is to be cremated and then it will be too late to do anything."

"All the more reason we should move fast to find Lucy," grated Shayne. "Who do you think wrote those notes?"

"They sound like Charles."

"That's what I thought. But I've got reason to think Charles wasn't physically capable of snatching Lucy. Who else among those you suspect?"

"Any one of them. Or all of them put together. If Charles didn't write the notes, I'd guess it was someone else who tried to make them sound like Charles."

"You mean Marvin, Anita, Mrs. Blair and the doctor."

"And don't forget Harold Peabody. Cold as a fish and sharp as a hound's tooth. He's got more brains in his little finger than all the others put together. Wouldn't surprise me one little bit if he engineered the whole deal from the word go."

"What do you mean?"

"Just what I say. That he put Anita up to it from the very beginning. Fixed it for John to meet her in the first place, hoping he'd fall for her like he did. She was working in his office, you know. I don't trust that man half as far as I could throw a bull by the tail, and I've told John so hundreds of times. I think John was beginning to catch on and he was scared he was going to lose John's business and that would involve a complete audit . . . and only Harold Peabody knows what an audit would show.

"I told John over and over that he was a fool to give Peabody a free hand with his investments and that I bet he was stealing him blind, but John trusted him. Until lately. But I think he was beginning to get suspicious and Peabody knew it. If John was pressing him for an outside audit he'd have a mighty strong motive for seeing John died when he did."

"That motive doesn't stand up," Shayne pointed out. "With your brother's death there will be an automatic audit of his accounts and appraisal of his estate . . . for tax purposes, if nothing else. This is the one thing Peabody would want to avoid if your suspicion is correct and there are any irregularities."

"Oh, no. Give the devil his due. The way Harold Peabody has got things fixed, he's named executor of the estate and will have his finger in whatever audit or appraisal there is. Don't think that man hasn't got every angle figured."

"What are the terms of his will?"

"Just what you might expect an old fool to do," she said acidly. "Fifty thousand to Mrs. Blair and a trust fund for me that I can only spend the interest on. The rest of it to his dearly beloved wife, Anita, with no strings attached. And my trust fund also goes to her when I die."

"When you brought the suit, did you anticipate something like this?"

"John was a man . . . and I know how men are. Some little slut comes along and lifts her skirt, and he goes panting after her. That's exactly what happened when Harold Peabody fixed it for Anita to lift her skirt for my brother."

"You really think," said Shayne incredulously, "that a man with Peabody's reputation deliberately planned to introduce Anita to your brother, hoping he would marry her so that she could then murder him and gain control of his fortune?"

"I won't argue with you about his reputation," she said tartly. "But it wouldn't be the first time something like that has happened."

"You think he's the type to pull something like that with Lucy?"

"I consider him utterly unscrupulous. If he found out you were digging the dog up to have it analyzed, I'm sure he'd stop at nothing to stop you. How *did* you find Daffy?"

Shayne said, "That's a trade secret."

"Now that you have got her body, you're not just going to sit back and do nothing because of these threats."

Shayne said stubbornly, "The moment Lucy is safe, I'll start moving."

"How much?" she demanded suddenly.

"How much what?"

"How much do you intend to hold me up for? I know a lot about you, Mike Shayne, and I don't believe for a minute that any woman means more to you than money. How much for immediate delivery of Daffy's body to me? Then your conscience will be clear. You can wash your hands of the whole affair and devote your entire time to getting your secretary back safe and sound of limb."

Shayne got up. He took a step forward and caught the slip of yellow paper from her fingers. He carefully folded it together with the note she had given him. In a remote voice, he said:

"I'll keep both of these. And I'll also keep Daffy. Good night."

He stalked out of the hotel suite

and shut the door firmly behind him.

In the lobby he looked for Harold Peabody in the telephone book and found his home address in the northeast section of the city. He made a note of it and went out to a waiting cab and told the driver to take him to the fishing dock where he had left his car parked earlier that day.

The telephone was ringing when Shayne let himself into his apartment. He lifted it quickly and said, "Hello."

Lucy Hamilton's voice came over the wire, without the familiar lilt in it, but calm and steady and purposeful:

"Michael. Just listen to me and don't ask questions. I'm *all right*. They won't harm me if you drop the Rogell case . . . don't have the dog's stomach analyzed. I will be released tomorrow afternoon if the funeral goes off on schedule." Her calm rendition of prepared lines changed to staccato intensity. "Don't pay any attention . . ."

There was a click and then silence. Shayne's hand was unsteady as he replaced the receiver. Subconsciously, he had expected her call. Whoever was holding Lucy would be smart enough to know the only pressure that could be exerted on the detective would be his belief that she was safe and would be released safely if he followed orders. On the other hand, how many kidnap victims *were* re-turned safe after the ransom was paid?

He got up and paced restlessly up and down the room. He should, of course, take the kidnap notes to Will Gentry at once—throw the entire resources of the police department into the search for her and her abductor.

But he knew he wasn't going to do that. Once the alarm was out, Lucy's life wouldn't be worth a plugged nickel. Alone, he could accomplish exactly as much as the police department. Which was exactly nothing.

Yet he knew he had to try. He couldn't just sit and wait for the autopsy report. He was already positive in his own mind that the finding would be murder. There was no other possible reason for Lucy being snatched. He decided the Shamrock was worth another try.

Shayne had his coat on and was headed toward the door by the time he got that far in his theorizing.

The bar was still open when he got there the second time. The same bartender was still listlessly on duty, and now there were five bar-stools occupied, two of them by women who were giggling with three men eager to buy them drinks.

The bartender recognized the redhead, and glanced inquiringly toward the bottle of cognac behind him. Shayne nodded and the man poured out a drink and remembered to put a glass of water beside it. He leaned his forearms on the bar and asked, "You get a line of that fellow you was asking about?"

Shayne shook his head. "That's why I'm back. To see if you can remember another damned thing about him that might help."

"Sorry, Mister. I told you all I could the first time."

"Think hard. Maybe you might have noticed a stranger that came in about the same time the bum did. Stayed for a drink or two while he was here, and then went out after he left."

"See what you mean," mumbled the bartender, wrinkling his forehead deeper and half-closing his eyes in deep concentration. "Another guy keeping an eye on him, to make sure he called Western Union and the notes got left with me?"

"That's it exactly. Keep this up and I'll get you a detective rating on the police force."

Obviously pleased, the man continued his effort to concentrate while Shayne sipped at his drink and waited hopefully. Finally, he shook his head. "It just don't come. I been thinking back hard, but it just don't come, Mister. There was a pretty good crowd in here. Some that I never saw before. But I don't recollect any one of 'em paying any particular heed to this bum."

"Keep on thinking," Shayne urged him. "Here's a couple of descriptions." He described Charles first, ending, "You'd have noticed him for sure. Two front teeth freshly knocked out and the side of his face split, with probably a bandage on it."

The man shook his head decisively. "I'd remember him for sure. Nobody like that."

Shayne said without much hope, "Try these two on for size." He described Harold Peabody and Marvin Dale as best he could, realizing as he did so how commonplace both were, and how unlikely to arouse any particular notice from a busy bartender.

When the man again shook him head regretfully, Shayne finished his drink briskly and shoved a five across the counter. "Thanks for trying," he said.

When he left the bar Shayne realized he had accomplished exactly nothing. But he had tried.

Back in his own room, he walked past the cognac bottle on the center table into the small kitchen and put a teakettle of water to heat. Then he sat down in the livingroom with a mug of strong black coffee and waited for his telephone to ring.

IX

SHAYNE DRESSED IN fresh clothes while he waited, and when the telephone finally did ring it was Will Gentry as he anticipated.

"I just got the autopsy report, Mike."

"And?"

"John Rogell died of heart failure."

The tenseness went out of Shayne and he clawed at his red hair happily. "Thank God for that. No question about it?"

Gentry said soberly, "Forgive me for giving you a wrong impression Mike. He died because his heart stopped beating . . . because he ingested at least a teaspoonful of tincture of digitalis within half an hour before he died."

Shayne said, "Goddamn it, Will. There's something you don't know. I had a telephone call from her last night . . . to say she was okay and would be okay if the autopsy weren't done and the funeral went off without any hitch."

"Do you believe it, Mike?"

"As much as I believe any vicious kidnapper." Shayne's voice was harsh with strain. "I know what the odds are, but that makes no difference."

"Hell, I'm as worried about Lucy as you are," Gentry said. "On the other hand, Mike . . . now we've got definite proof Rogell was murdered by someone in the house that evening. We'll work as quietly as possible, but . . ."

"Tell me about the digitalis," Shayne interrupted. "Isn't that a regular medicine for the heart?"

"Sure. Rogell had been on the stuff for years. A daily dose of twelve drops had been keeping him alive. Doctor Jenson prescribed it first, and the new fellow . . . Evans . . . kept the dosage the same."

"How could they get the old man to take so large a dose?"

"That was the easiest part of it, Mike. Here's the complete picture as we have it now. His wife always administered the twelve drops personally about midnight before he went to sleep. She gave it to him in a cup of hot chocolate milk which the housekeeper prepared in the kitchen each evening and put in a thermos jug downstairs before she retired. This would have been common household knowledge, of course. The medicine bottle was kept in the bathroom shared by Rogell and his wife. Anita could have poured an extra teaspoonful in his milk on that particular night . . . or just about anyone else in the house could have got hold of the bottle and slipped it into the thermos jug downstairs."

"That leaves it nice and wide open," said Shayne bitterly.

"Right. Now I want to know what in hell you're doing about Lucy."

Shayne said, "I've got to talk to you, Will. Don't make a move until I see you. And can you have the detectives on tap who went out to Rogell's that night?"

"I will. But, Mike! Don't expect

me to sit on this. We've got a poisoner who has killed once, and made a second attempt."

"And he or she has got Lucy," Shayne reminded him grimly.

Gentry said with heavy finality, "I'll be waiting for you in my office," and hung up.

As the result of a telephone call, Timothy Rourke met the detective at a side entrance to police headquarters. They paused outside while Shayne briefly explained the latest developments to Rourke, and then they went in to Gentry's private office together.

Shayne wasted no time in idle talk. He got out the two sheets of yellow paper and laid them in front of Gentry. "These were delivered to me and Miss Henrietta about midnight last night. By a messenger who'd picked them up at a Miami Avenue bar."

He went on to describe their visit to the Shamrock Bar while Will Gentry read the two notes.

"I went straight to Lucy's place, Will, and found she'd been there a couple of hours during the evening . . . probably after dinner . . . and had left hurriedly. I'm sure she didn't know *why* she was leaving because there was nothing left for me. Then there was the phone call from her later that I told you about."

Chief Gentry had curiously rumpled eyelids which he habitually raised and lowered much in the manner of venetian blinds. He leaned back in his chair and folded them up as he demanded:

"Who out at the Rogell place knew you had dug up the dog's body. How did they know *you* did it . . . and how to get at Lucy?"

Shayne lit a cigarette and briefly recounted the ruse he had employed to discover where Daffy was buried, and how he and Tim had gotten possession of the body.

"They guessed why I was there at night, of course," he concluded, "and after I left with Dr. Evans somebody must have checked Daffy's grave. How they knew how to get to Lucy, I don't know. But someone was desperate enough to kidnap her to try and stop me from having the dog's stomach contents analyzed."

"The chauffeur sounds most likely," rumbled Gentry.

"I know. The two notes sound like him. But I knocked hell out of him, Will, and Mrs. Blair swears he went to bed at once in his own room over the garage with a sedative strong enough to put him out for eight hours."

"The widow and her brother?" demanded Gentry.

"I swear I don't know. The brother appears weak, and was pretty drunk. Anita is . . . capable of anything. On the other hand, Henrietta plugs for Harold Peabody as the mastermind. And I wouldn't put anything past so cold-blooded a guy. But guessing is no good," he went on somberly. "Someone has Lucy put away on ice, and all we can hope right now is that they think I'm sufficiently scared to not have the dog analyzed."

Gentry leaned back with a sigh and rolled his sodden cigar from one corner of his mouth to the other. "You think she'll be safe as long as they think that?"

"Until after the funeral anyhow." Shayne met his gaze squarely. "If you don't upset the applecart by doing anything to indicate the Rogell case is being reopened."

"And after the funeral?"

Shayne shook his red head and said doggedly, "If it goes off all right and the killer thinks Rogell is safely cremated and all proof of murder has gone up in smoke, I think there's a chance Lucy will be released."

"Or?" asked Gentry significantly.

"Or killed," Shayne said bluntly, the trenches deep in his cheeks. "But they'll keep her safe until after the funeral, Will, and I want that much time with no official interference."

"You're asking me to sit on a murder."

"A murder you wouldn't know a damned thing about if I hadn't handed it to you on a silver platter," flared Shayne.

Gentry said soothingly, "Sure, Mike. I grant you that. Sure, I'll give you all the time you want," he added generously. "Up until . . . say . . . three o'clock this afternoon."

"That ought to be plenty," said Shayne bitterly, "for me to solve a murder that the whole goddamn police force of Miami has had in their lap for several days." He got up and demanded abruptly, "Where'll I find Petrie and Donovan?"

"They're waiting for you right inside." Will Gentry gestured toward a closed door. "I've told them to give you everything, Mike, and in addition to that, they're under your orders if you want to make use of them."

"Until three o'clock?"

Gentry said, "Until three o'clock," and Shayne jerked his head at Rourke and went to the side door to interview the two detectives who had handled the Rogell investigation.

Shayne and Rourke both knew the two city detectives casually, and the men greeted them without particular enthusiasm as they entered. Petrie was thin and sour-faced, and he said sneeringly, "Gentry tells us you're going to turn the Rogell thing into murder . . . and then solve it for us."

Donovan was flabby-fat and easy-going. He grinned amiably and told them, "Don't pay no heed to Jim. He's sore because the chief wouldn't let him haul in that hot little dish of a widow and give her a going-over. Not that I wouldn't like to work over her myself, if you get what I mean." He rolled his eyes and smacked his lips suggestively.

Shayne said, "Why don't you two start by telling us exactly what happened the night Rogell died."

With Petrie doing most of the talking and Donovan filling in some details, they related how they had been called to the Rogell house by an insistent telephone call received from his sister at twelve-forty, which was exactly eleven minutes after her millionaire brother had died quietly in his bed.

On arrival, they had been met at the door by Henrietta, fully-clothed and tearless, loudly insisting that she was convinced John Rogell had been poisoned by his wife. In the small library off the right of the hall, they had found Marvin Dale, soddenly drunk and obviously quite pleased that his brother-in-law had passed on. With Marvin had been Harold Peabody, sober and shaken, who told them he had spent the latter part of the evening alone with the millionaire in his second-floor sitting room, going over business affairs with him until Anita had interrupted them precisely at midnight with a hot drink for her husband which she invariably brought to him each night at that hour.

It had been a normal evening, Peabody insisted, with Rogell in the best of spirits and apparently in perfect physical condition, and

he had left husband and wife together at twelve with no premonition of what was to come, had paused in the library for a nightcap with Marvin, and they were together when Anita called down frantically that John had had a stroke and to call Dr. Evans immediately.

The doctor had arrived within ten minutes and found his patient already dead. He was upstairs with the body when the detectives went up, and had not the slightest hesitancy in positively declaring that death was the normal result of Rogell's heart condition, and had signed the death certificate to that effect.

Mrs. Blair, the housekeeper, had been in Anita's boudoir consoling the grief-stricken widow whom they found fetchingly attired in a lacy nightgown and filmy black negligee. Mrs. Blair was also wearing slippers and robe, and told the officers she had retired to her third-floor quarters about eleven as was her custom, after preparing a silver thermos pitcher of hot chocolate milk for Mr. Rogell and leaving it downstairs on a tray on the dining table for Anita to take up to him at midnight . . . a nightly service which she insisted on performing for him herself every night.

In a highly emotional state and with much sobbing, Anita had related how John had appeared in good spirits when she entered the

room with his tray and shooed
Peabody out. Her husband was already in pajamas and robe, she
told them, and she poured out his
hot drink herself and sat with him
while he drank it. Then she had
gone into his separate bedroom
with him. She was standing by the
dresser when he'd groaned and
stiffened in his bed, and a moment
later his body became rigid and his
breathing shallow and fast.

It was then she had run to the
head of the stairs to shout for the
doctor, and when she returned to
the bedroom a moment later, she
could no longer detect his breathing. Henrietta had then come in
from her own suite at the end of the
hallway, and angrily berated her
for being an unfaithful wife . . .
then gone on to an open accusation
of murder.

"What's the use kicking it around
now?" demanded Petrie. "The old
boy is going to be burned to a
crisp at noon, and if there ever was
any evidence of murder inside him,
it'll be destroyed."

"That's why we've got to move
fast," said Shayne with a driving
intensity behind his words. He
glanced at his watch and calculated swiftly that it was just a few
minutes before eight o'clock in
Denver, Colorado. He dragged a
worn address book from his pocket
and checked an old entry, then
told the others, "Sit tight right
here. I'm going to make a fast
phone call from Gentry's office, and

then we'll all get on our horses."

He strode through the connecting door and found Gentry talking
to a young patrolman who stood
stiffly at attention beside the
chief's desk. Shayne said, "I've got
to make a call, Will," picked up a
telephone from his desk and got
the police operator. He said crisply, "Person-to-person in Denver,
Colorado. Felix Ritter. Here's an
old telephone number I have for
him."

He read the number from his
book and lowered one hip to the
corner of Gentry's desk while he
waited. Impersonally, and with
only a tiny part of his mind, he
listened to Chief Gentry chewing
out the patrolman for some minor
infraction of regulations while the
long distance connection was being made, and when he heard Ritter's voice on the other end, he
said incisively:

"Mike Shayne in Miami, Felix.
Can you get out to Central City
fast?"

"Mike? Sure I can. There's a
new road since you were here."

"Fast as you can make it," said
Shayne. "Write this down. I want
any gossip or scandal from the
natives about a Mrs. Betty Blair
who used to run a rooming house
there where the millionaire miner,
John Rogell, hung out while he
was making his fortune. Find out
how friendly they were in the old
days . . . and what people
thought when Mr. Blair died and

the widow came to Miami to work as John Rogell's housekeeper. Got it. Here's an angle. He left her fifty thousand bucks in his will."

"Sure, Mike. Rogell just died, huh? In Miami? Remember reading how he got his start in Central City."

"Fast as you can make it, Felix. I need any damned thing you can pick up and relay to me by twelve o'clock. Make a collect call to the Chief of Police here. Will Gentry. Before noon."

Felix Ritter in Denver said, "Will do," and Shayne hung up.

The patrolman was on his way out, and Shayne told Gentry, "You'll be getting a call about Mrs. Blair from Central City before noon. I'll be checking with you about that time. If you'll have it ready to read off to me—"

Another telephone on Gentry's desk interrupted him. The chief scooped it up and said, "Yes?" He listened a moment, lifting a beefy hand at Shayne, his rumpled eyelids moving up and down slowly. He hung up and told Shayne, "Let's get out to the Rogell place with Petrie and Donovan. Marvin Dale committed suicide out there last night. And left a suicide note addressed to you."

X

IN SHAYNE'S CAR, he and Rourke followed the screaming siren of Chief Gentry's limousine through downtown traffic and out Brickel Boulevard to the Rogell estate.

A white-faced maid opened the door for them immediately, and Mrs. Blair hovered in the wide hallway behind her, wringing her hands and with tearstreaks on her broad face.

"This way," she directed them. "Up the stairs here. I just can't believe it. Poor Mr. Dale. Who'd ever have thought he'd do a terrible thing like this."

The five men trooped beside her silently up the curving stairway where she turned to the right to an open doorway with Charles standing in front of it. He was in his shirtsleeves and without a tie, his hair uncombed and a heavy growth of dark stubble on his square face. There was a bluish bruise on his cheekbone and a pad of gauze on the side of his mouth under a piece of surgical tape.

He kept his lips pressed tightly together and his eyes had a sullen glare when he saw Shayne with the others. He stepped aside from the doorway without speaking, and they entered a medium-sized bedroom with the body of Marvin Dale sprawled on the floor in front of a drop-leaf table with an overturned straight chair beside him.

The young man's face was twisted and ghastly in death, his body stiffly contorted, indicating that he had writhed agonizingly on the floor before death mercifully ended his suffering.

There was a bottle of whiskey standing on the table, with a highball glass beside it. The glass held a small residue of brownish liquid. Off to one side was a small, round, squat bottle with the warning skull and crossbones plainly imprinted on it. It was labeled *"Strychnine"*, and there was also the word *"Poison"* in large type.

Beside the bottle of strychnine were two torn pieces of notepaper that had been crumpled up and then smoothed and carefully placed one above the other, with torn edges in juxtaposition so that a superficial glance indicated that they were the torn top and bottom pieces of the same sheet of notepaper. A square box of the same notepaper and a ballpoint pen were on the extreme left-hand side of the table.

While Gentry and the two detectives knelt beside Marvin Dale's body, Shayne leaned over the table to read the scrawled handwriting on the sheet of torn notepaper:

Michael Shayne—
I will write this note while I can. I love my sister and have always forgiven her anything she did because I was too weak to protest, but I can't go on
any longer. She is a sweet girl and after seeing her with Charles tonight I am revolted. Death holds no fear for me. John and Henrietta were old and mean and deserved to die. But this thing tonight is the

last straw and I don't want to go on living.

Marvin Dale

Shayne read the torn note through without touching either half of it. Gentry got to his feet from beside the body with a sigh and said, "All the signs of typical strychnine poisoning. He's been dead for hours."

He stood beside Shayne and looked down at the note, mumbling the words half aloud as he read them. Then he turned to the doorway and ordered the chauffeur curtly, "Come in here."

Charles walked in with his chin up and shoulders squared.

"Who are you?"

"Charles Morton. The chauffeur."

"What do you know about this?"

"He hasn't been touched," Charles said stolidly. "Nothing has been touched . . ." He paused and his gaze flickered down to the table and the torn note. ". . . except that piece of paper. Mrs. Rogell discovered her brother's body about nine o'clock. The note was lying on the table . . . all in one piece. She called me in from my rooms over the garage and showed it to me. She wanted to tear it up before she called the police. I told her we couldn't destroy suicide evidence and tried to snatch it from her. It got torn and crumpled as you see it, but I insisted the police had to see it . . . no matter what inter-

pretation you put on what Marvin said."

"Very cooperative and law-abiding of you," said Gentry harshly. He turned his gaze back to the torn paper and read aloud, "She is a sweet girl and after seeing her with Charles tonight I am utterly revolted. How do you expect me to interpret that?"

"In the very nastiest way possible, I'm sure," said Charles steadily.

"How do you explain it?"

"Marvin was drunk last night. No drunker than usual, but . . . staggering. After I had retired with a couple of pills Dr. Evans gave me, Mrs. Rogell became worried about my injuries and came out to the garage wearing her gown and nightrobe just to be sure I needed no further medical attention. In his drunken state, Marvin saw her going out the back door and followed her up to my bedroom. He burst in on us and made a nasty scene . . . accusing his sister of all sorts of wild things. Of course there was nothing in it. I chased him out, and then sent Mrs. Rogell back to the house. That's why she wanted to destroy the note before anyone read it. It might give some people false ideas."

"Do you think it's a confession that he killed Rogell and tried to poison Henrietta."

"I think that's for you to decide. Personally, I don't know that Mr.

Rogell was killed or that anyone tried to poison Miss Henrietta."

"Where did the strychnine come from?"

"I think it's a bottle from the garage that the gardener keeps for killing moles. It looks exactly like one that was always kept in the garage, and I checked after I saw it, and that bottle is gone."

"Then you want us to believe that Marvin was so upset by surprising his sister in your bed that he got this bottle of poison from the garage, brought it in and wrote that note, and then drank a dose of it?"

"I don't particularly want you to believe anything," countered Charles doggedly. "There he is and there's the note. I convinced Mrs. Rogell that it would be better to give you the note and tell you the exact truth instead of destroying it as she wanted to do."

"What happened to your face . . . and your two front teeth?" demanded Gentry.

Shayne said, "I jumped him while he was holding a cocked, double-barreled shotgun on me. It was self-defense. Marvin was pretty drunk that early in the evening while I was here, and he seemed determined to get a lot drunker. I don't see how he stayed sober enough to do this."

"He'd often drink so much he'd vomit it up and get sort of sober, and then start over," offered Charles.

There was the thin keening of a siren outside, and Gentry said, "That'll be the doc and the lab boys. Stay in here, Donovan. Petrie, you take this fellow downstairs and hold him. I want to talk to Mrs. Rogell."

Gentry shook his head soberly as they climbed the stairs to interview Anita Rogell. "I don't like any of this, Mike. There's a stink I can't get out of my nostrils." He stopped at the head of the stairs abruptly and suggested, "Let's see what Doc says before we talk to Mrs. Rogell."

Doc Higgens had completed his examination and he came out of the death room briskly as they turned toward it. He said, "A massive dose of strychnine—until I do a P.M.—taken in a highball about eight hours ago. Send him down to my charnelhouse as soon as you're through with him."

He went on, and Chief Gentry went into the room to confer with his technicians, and Timothy Rourke sauntered out and rejoined Shayne.

"They sure it's his handwriting . . . and the two torn pieces check?" Shayne asked.

"They check perfectly," Tim said. "Couldn't possibly be faked. And George, the identification man, found a lot of samples of Marvin's writing and swears it's the same . . . though the man was obviously pretty drunk when he wrote the note."

"He'd have to be to calmly swallow strychnine. Which is probably why the note isn't more rational. Very few suicide notes are wholly rational," Shayne went on with a frown, as though arguing a point with himself. "By the time they work themselves up to that point, they're not making too much sense. On the other hand, I've got a strange feeling about the wording of that note.

GETTING OFF THE elevator, Michael Shayne strode across the hall and mechanically reached for the knob of the door lettered: MICHAEL SHAYNE—*Investigations*.

The knob turned but the door refused to open. He cursed himself methodically and in a low voice because he had forgotten momentarily that Lucy Hamilton would not be inside the office waiting for him, and he unlocked the door and flung it open with savage force.

He strode across the office to his desk, lifted the telephone and dialled Chief Will Gentry's private number at police headquarters.

When Gentry answered, he asked briskly, "Any long distance calls for me, Will? From Colorado particularly?"

"Your man called here a little before twelve," Gentry told him. "He got hold of nothing positive in Central City except ancient gossip and strong suspicions among the townfolk that John Rogell and

Betty Blair did have an affair in the old days. It was revived when he hired her to come to Miami as his housekeeper, and the town is buzzing again now that he's left her that hunk of cash in his will. One other small thing, Mike. A lot of oldtimers agree that Henrietta was the aggressive, strong one in the early days, and that it was her vigor and drive that laid the groundwork for the Rogell fortune."

"Funeral going off all right?" asked the redhead.

"So far as I know. I've got four men covering it and they haven't reported anything. Goddamn it, Mike! I think it's time we stepped in. If Lucy is . . ."

"You promised me until three o'clock." Beads of sweat had formed on Shayne's forehead and were coursing down the trenches in his cheeks.

"I know I did, you stubborn Mick. But I don't see . . ."

"I don't either," Shayne interrupted him much more calmly than he felt. "I'm coming over, Will. I can't just sit here."

He dropped the receiver and slowly got to his feet. His glance fell on the half-filled cup on his desk and he reached for it, checked his big hand before he touched it and hesitated a long moment.

Then his lips came back from his teeth in a terrifying sort of grin, and he swept up the twin cups and downed the liquor in two gulps. He was getting childish, by God. Or senile, maybe. Any time Mike Shayne walked out of his office and left a half-finished drink on his desk it would be time for him to turn in his license.

And maybe it was at that.

But not quite yet. Not until three o'clock.

Not until he was convinced that Lucy—

CHIEF WILL GENTRY was seated alone at his desk stolidly munching on a ham sandwich and sipping from a container of black coffee when Shayne walked in. There were some typewritten sheets shoved back carelessly in front of him, and beside his right hand lay Marvin Dale's suicide note. Back from that was the box of notepaper and the ballpoint pen with which the note had been written.

Gentry looked up from studying the note with an impatient shrug of his broad shoulders. "Can't keep my eyes off this thing," he muttered. "Keep reading it over and over with the feeling it's trying to say *something* to me that I don't get."

He stared levelly at Shayne.

Shayne nodded, hooking his toe under the rung of a straight chair and dragging it close to the side of the chief's desk. "I know. It's a hunch that won't break through." He closed his eyes and recited the contents of the note, spacing the words carefully and avoiding giving any one of them special emphasis:

"I will write this note while I can. I love my sister and have always forgiven her anything she did because I was too weak to protest, but I can't go on any longer. She is a sweet girl and after seeing her with Charles tonight I am revolted. Death holds no fears for me. John and Henrietta were old and mean and deserved to die. But this thing tonight is the last straw and I don't want to go on living. Marvin Dale."

He stopped speaking and the words hung in the silent air between the two men. Gentry took a gulp of coffee and wiped his thick lips with the back of his hand.

"Boil it right down, Mike, it doesn't *say* anything. You keep thinking it must make sense and each sentence seems like it does, but when you add it up . . . what do you get?"

Shayne said, "I know what you mean." He lit a cigarette and leaned forward, narrowing his eyes at the note, the torn halves placed in perfect juxtaposition and fastened with scotch tape. His right hand reached out and toyed with the octagonal ballpoint pen which the experts declared had written the note. "No fingerprints on this thing, I suppose."

"You know better'n that, Mike. Sure, there was a whorl or two. But what the hell? You know all the chemical tests they got. That pen wrote the note . . . and it's Marvin Dale's handwriting."

"On a sheet of paper out of this box." Shayne idly lifted a sheet between thumb and forefinger and weighed it thoughtfully. It was thick, and somewhat creamy in color, a single unfolded sheet about five by eight inches in size, obviously expensive, but with no monogram or engraved heading.

He stared at it for a long time, with blue smoke curling up from the tip of his cigarette past his narrowed eyes. A curiously blank expression spread over his rugged features, much as though a sort of self-hypnosis gripped him, and then very carefully, very deliberately, he placed the blank sheet of paper exactly beside the mended note, meticulously lining up the two edges so they touched, and putting the top edges in perfect alignment.

In an absolutely flat voice, he said, "Got it, Will. We should both have our heads examined."

"What you got?" Gentry craned his neck to look.

Shayne's forefinger stabbed down decisively to the bottom edges of the two sheets, mutely pointing out the fact that the sheet on which the note was written was a good quarter inch shorter than the unused sheet he had placed beside it.

"But they can't be different!" exploded Gentry. "Same watermark and same thickness and color.

They ran all sorts of tests. . . ."

"But not the same size sheet," Shayne pointed out. "That's the one simple test your experts didn't think about making, Will."

"Even if it didn't come from that same box, I don't see what it gets us," grumbled Gentry. "It's still in Dale's handwriting, and so . . ."

"I think I know exactly where it gets us." Shayne's voice was harsh with assurance. "Don't you get it yet? It *is* the same paper, but . . . when the torn halves were pasted back together it doesn't come out the same length."

"You mean there's one line missing out of the middle? One line that might change the whole meaning, if it was there? Yeah, but . . . but . . . Wait, Mike, Goddamnit! That can't be right either. Those rough edges absolutely coincide. Even under a microscope. If they'd been torn twice in order to eliminate one line, they couldn't still match up."

Shayne said quietly, "Watch this, Will." He took two fresh sheets from the box and lined them up meticulously on the desk so one lay exactly on top of the other. Then he gently moved the top sheet down a quarter of an inch, keeping the edges in alignment. Placing the palm of his left hand solidly across the lower portion of the two sheets so neither one could move, he took hold of the double edge between right thumb and forefinger and ripped the two sheets across just above the side of his hand.

Then he discarded the lower half of the top sheet and put it aside with the top half of the under sheet. He asked, "Got any scotch tape?" and fitted the half of the top sheet exactly together with the torn edge of the half of the lower sheet.

Gentry jerked open a drawer and got out a spool of tape, ripped off a small piece and fastened the two halves of the different sheets together while Shayne held them carefully.

Shayne said grimly, "There we are. Two torn halves that fit together so perfectly that a microscope couldn't detect anything. But just about a quarter inch shorter than the original size."

"The top and bottom parts of two different notes . . . torn across like you did so they match. But how in hell did the wording ever match up?" Gentry shifted his gaze to the note. "The top part doesn't even end with a period. The sentence goes right on to the next part."

"Looking just as though it was intended to be that way," agreed Shayne. "That must have been pure coincidence. One that somebody noticed and was smart enough to take advantage of after he read both notes and realized the two parts could be made to sound like the same one, if no one suspected differently."

"Why two notes? Both in Dale's handwriting?"

Shayne shrugged. "Two drafts of the same note, maybe. The guy was drunk and under a lot of stress. Maybe he had some reason to write two notes. The second one might even have been addressed to someone else."

"Then we'll never know what they really said when placed in the right order. This discovery won't help us at all."

"Maybe not. But we do know damned well that both Charles and Anita were lying when they told us how the note got torn." Shayne glanced at his watch, his eyes glittering with excitement. "That funeral ought to be about over. I want to be out there at the house when they get back." He drummed the tips of his fingers on the desk, thinking hard.

"Have you got Harold Peabody's office number?"

"It's here some place in some notes." Gentry scrabbled among the papers, found a list of names and addresses and read off the number to Shayne.

The detective dialled it, and when a woman's voice answered, he asked for Mr. Peabody.

"I'm sorry he isn't in just now. Could someone else be of help?"

Shayne said, "No. It's a personal matter. When do you expect him?"

"Well, he's attending a funeral, and I'm not sure . . ."

"Rogell. Of course," said Shayne

heartily. "Do you know what Mr. Peabody planned to do afterward?"

"Why, yes." The voice was noticeably warmer. "I believe he planned to go straight on out with Mrs. Rogell to hear the will read."

Shayne breathed, "Thanks, honey," and hung up. He leaped to his feet and told Gentry:

"Have Petrie and Donovan meet me at Rogell's fast as they can make it." He snatched up the note addressed to him and shoved it in his pocket, went out of the office fast.

XI

THEY WERE ALL there to hear John Rogell's will read, Shayne noted with satisfaction. Anita and Charles and Henrietta and Mrs. Blair. And Harold Peabody hovering behind Anita's chair, and an elderly man who was a stranger to him seated apart from the others with a legal-sized folder of papers bound in blue cardboard open on his knees.

They all stared at Shayne in silence and in varying degrees of surprise, apprehension and defiance as he walked into the room and looked from one face to another.

Harold Peabody spoke first. He straightened his body into a sort of strut behind Anita's chair, and spoke acidly, "This is a private conference, Mr. Shayne."

"And I'm a private detective," growled the redhead. He looked toward the elderly man who was obviously a lawyer and said, "Sorry to interrupt your proceedings, but I don't think this will take very long."

He advanced toward Anita who shrank back from him in the depths of a big chair and looked small and defenceless, and stood towering over her as he said mercilessly, "I want the truth about this note signed by your brother's name." His hand came out of his pocket holding the crumpled note and he waved it in front of her face.

"I know you lied about it," he told her conversationally. "I know you didn't find it lying beside his body as you said, and I know it didn't get torn in half the way you told me it did. Hell," he went on in a tone of utter disgust, "it's perfectly evident that this is two halves of two different notes. The only thing I *don't* know is what each note said when put together correctly, but I've got a damned good idea that both of them contained evidence that you murdered your husband, and that's why you got Charles to lie for you to help you pass this off as a real note."

"Don't answer him, Anita." The chauffeur was on his feet instantly, his voice thick with rage. "He's trying to trick you. He don't know . . ."

Shayne didn't glance aside. He

said sharply, "Shut him up, Donovan."

The big detective moved behind him swiftly with drawn revolver and Shayne continued to stand over Anita with his eyes boring into hers.

"If the original notes didn't say that, you'd better tell us what they *did* say. You've covered up for Charles as far as you can," he went on remorselessly. "Now you'd better start thinking about your own neck. Or maybe it's too late for that. Was it *you* who killed your own brother after you realized you could fix a note so it'd look like suicide?"

"No, no!" she cried in a strangled voice. "It was Charles. He told me . . ."

She was interrupted by a shout from Charles, a muttered oath from Donovan and the solid clunk of a revolver barrel against flesh and bone. This was followed by the heavy thump of a solid body against the floor, and Shayne turned his head to see Donovan kneeling over Charles' recumbent figure and snapping handcuffs on the man's lax wrists.

Shayne turned back to the widow dispassionately, "He won't make any further trouble. Tell us what happened."

"I want to," she sobbed. "I wanted to all the time, but he frightened me. He showed me Marvin's two notes and they did sound like he thought I'd killed

John and tried to poison Henrietta. And he showed me how it'd work if we tore them apart in just the right place and put the two wrong halves together. And we made up that story about Marvin catching us together in his room so the note would make sense that way.

"And Marvin was already dead," she wept on, hanging her head piteously. "I guess I really knew Charles had done it after frightening him into writing those two notes, but I was so scared and upset after what happened to Daffy and all that I hardly knew what I was doing."

"You say there were two notes originally. Addressed to whom?"

"One was written to you and one to me," she told him faintly. "He meant to hide them someplace in the hope that one of them would be found, I guess."

"But Charles got hold of them before he had a chance to hide them?" put in Shayne harshly.

"Yes. I guess so."

"What did the original notes say?"

"I remember every word of the one written to me." Anita shuddered and hung her head.

"What did he say?"

He started out: 'Dear Sis'." She lifted her chin and recited tonelessly:

"If Charles kills me tonight as I expect him to, I hope this note or one I'm writing to Mike Shayne and hiding in different places will be found. I kept quiet after I suspected you and Charles of murdering your husband, but after he kidnapped that nice secretary of Shayne's tonight and boasted to me that he plans to kill her after the funeral tomorrow, I can't remain silent any longer. She is a sweet girl and after seeing her with Charles tonight, I am revolted. Death holds no fears for me. John and Henrietta were old and mean and deserved to die. But this thing tonight is the last straw and I don't want to go on living. And his name was signed to it," she ended, tears running down her cheeks.

Shayne said, "And my note began: I will write this note while I can. I love my sister and have always forgiven her anything she did because I was too weak to protest, but I can't go on . . ."

He broke off, nodding his head understandingly. "That was the end of a line. He took the note from his pocket and looked at it.

"Fortuitously, the first two words of a line down in the middle of your note were, 'any longer'. By tearing the two notes across between those two lines, the final note read as though the same thought was being carried on . . . with the implication that Marvin intended to kill himself instead of voicing his fear that Charles planned to kill him. Very neat. And so you went along with the deception?"

"What else could I do?" she sobbed frantically. "Charles practically admitted he had killed Marvin, and he threatened to kill me, too, unless I . . ."

"You damned lying bitch!" Charles was sitting upright on the floor with his wrists handcuffed behind him. His eyes were wild and there were bubbles of gray froth on his lips. "I did it all for you, goddamnit, after they dug up your lousy dog and I knew they'd find your strychnine in her belly that you'd meant for Henrietta. I told you last night why I grabbed the girl. Because I found the strychnine in your own handbag after you'd put it in Henrietta's chicken to shut her up."

"And I told you I *didn't* do it," she screamed at him, thrusting herself up from the depths of her chair. "I never saw the strychnine and I didn't do anything to John."

Shayne thrust her back into the chair savagely and said, "To hell with all that. You were talking about Lucy Hamilton. *What* did Charles do to her? *Where is she?*"

"In the boathouse. She was in the boathouse last night. But he said . . ."

Shayne whirled away from her and shot out at Petrie and Donovan, "Hold everything like it is." He pounded down the hallway and out through the kitchen door, across the parking lot and past the garage to the path leading to the boathouse at the foot of the cliff.

Two minutes later he was putting his shoulder to the door. The weathered wood splintered and gave way, and Shayne stepped through a gaping hole to see a neat Chris-Craft tied fore and aft in front of him with enough slack in the ropes so it could rise and fall with the bay tide.

He found an electric switch beside the smashed door and thumbed it, and an overhead light came on and he saw the figure of a girl huddled forlornly in one corner with a ragged blanket thrown over her.

He took two strides and snatched the blanket away from Lucy Hamilton's body, saw that she was fully-clothed, lying on her side with her body drawn into a bow with wrists tied tightly to her ankles, wide strips of adhesive tape tightly over her mouth.

Her eyes were wide open and unblinking, staring up at him, and he dropped to his knees beside her, choking back an oath and telling her cheerfully, "The marines have landed, angel."

He cut the rope binding her wrists to her ankles and eased her back gently onto the rough boards, rubbing the constricted leg muscles and straightening one and then the other slowly and gently so normal circulation would be restored.

"This is going to hurt, angel." He placed the wide palm of his hand firmly on her forehead to hold her head solidly against the floor,

got a good grip on the loosened ends of tape and pulled it loose with one strong jerk.

She moaned agonizingly and he felt hot tears against his palm, and he gathered her up in his arms like a little child and pressed her face tightly against his chest and pressed his lips gently against her disarranged curls and murmured crazy things to her which both of them remembered a long time afterward.

When she was through trembling and through crying and was able to speak in a small voice that was still somewhat distorted by pain, he continued to hold her tightly in his arms and she answered the few questions he needed answers to.

"Are you all *right,* Lucy? You know what I mean?"

She whispered, "Yes."

"Who put you here?"

"Charles. He telephoned . . ."

"I don't care how he worked it," Shayne told her brusquely. "Save your breath for important things. Did Charles kill Rogell?"

"I don't think so. He and Marvin . . . talked. He told Marvin Anita did it, and he was doing this to save her."

"Did Marvin believe it?"

"I . . . think so. He was good, Michael. Don't blame Marvin. He was . . . drunk, but decent. He argued with Charles about me. He threatened to tell you."

Still holding her closely, Shayne

got to his feet and carried her out through the smashed wooden door into the sunlight. One arm crept around his neck tightly as he carried her up the stairs and around to the front of the house and his parked car. He opened the rear door and slid her inside gently onto the cushion and said, "Stretch out and try to relax. I'll send the maid out with a glass of water which you should sip on . . . and I'll be ready to drive you home in a few minutes. Think you can hold out?"

She opened her eyes and smiled tremulously up into his concerned face. "I can stand anything now." She let out a little sigh of contentment and her eyelids fluttered shut again.

THE TABLEAU HADN'T changed much when Shayne came back into the study. Petrie and Donovan stood on guard in the archway. Anita was still huddled in the same chair, and Charles sat on the floor with his wrists handcuffed behind him. Peabody had moved to the bar and was mixing a drink, and Henrietta had taken advantage of his absence to make herself a stiff highball. The lawyer still sat stiffly in his chair, his thin lips tightly compressed.

No one spoke as Shayne walked in between Petrie and Donovan. The big redhead's face was impassive as he strode across the room and stopped directly in front of Charles and looked down at him. The chauffeur tilted back his head to look up with a snarl of defiance, and Shayne leaned down slightly to hit him a full-swinging open-handed blow on the left cheek.

The sound of the impact was loud in the room, and the force of it knocked Charles sprawling onto his side. Still without speaking, Shayne leaned down farther and savagely jerked him back up to a sitting position, set himself solidly and swung another full-arm blow with his left hand. Charles went over in the other direction like a nine-pin and stayed there, and Anita began sobbing wildly in her chair.

Shayne jerked the chauffeur roughly erect again and said happily, "This is real good fun. Charles. I can keep it up all day without getting tired. You want to start talking?"

"I did it for her," he mumbled. "I knew if you found the strychnine in Daffy you'd be onto her for feeding the same stuff to the old man. I wasn't going to hurt the girl. All I wanted was to scare you off from an autopsy."

"But Marvin messed things up by catching you with Lucy and threatening to turn you in for kidnapping," said Shayne conversationally.

"Even when I *told* him it was just to protect his sister," complained Charles with every appearance of righteous anger. "I couldn't afford that . . . not right then . . . so I tried to scare him out of it. How was I to know the fool was drunk enough to kill himself?"

Shayne said, "I don't believe he was. *You* had the strychnine. Remember? You admitted finding it in Anita's pocketbook after you buried Daffy."

"That's a lousy lie," cried out Anita viciously. "I didn't either. I didn't touch any strychnine. Why would I? If it was in my pocketbook, somebody put it there just to throw suspicion on me."

Shayne paid no attention to her. "But you did have it," he reminded Charles. "How did Marvin get hold of it to commit suicide?"

"I gave it to him, that's why," Charles glared up at him sullenly. "To prove to him that his own sister had tried to poison Henrietta to shut her up. So the fool would get some sense in his head and let me handle it my own way."

Shayne said, "We won't worry too much about whether you fed the stuff to Marvin or he took it himself. Kidnapping is a capital offense and they can only burn you once."

He swung about, transferring his bland gaze to Henrietta who sat bolt upright in a straight chair. She was gripping her highball glass tightly in both bony hands.

"You hired me to do a certain job for you yesterday, Miss Rogell. I did it, so I have no further intention of returning the retainer you paid me. An autopsy was performed secretly on your brother last night." He held her gaze impassively. "All of you here will be interested to know that John Rogell died of heart failure . . . exactly as Dr. Evans stated on the death certificate."

A long-drawn sigh came from Anita's lips. She sat up straight and her eyes flamed contemptuously at Charles on the floor. "I told you so." Her voice was thin with rage. "But you wouldn't believe me. Your lousy ego made you think I'd done something to John . . . when I loved him all the time."

"See here, young man." Henrietta's heavy voice cut in unexpectedly. "What sort of nincompoop performed that autopsy on my brother?"

"The regular police surgeon. A very competent man."

"Competent, my foot! He's a bungling fool. Didn't he have brains enough to check for digitalis?"

"But it was common knowledge that your brother had been taking digitalis for years," protested Shayne. "He would naturally expect to find that in his system."

"Of course, he would. And that's exactly why he should have measured the quantity he swallowed the night he died. Didn't he realize that's exactly what his wife would use to kill him? Instead of strychnine or something obvious like that. Mrs. Blair will bear me out that she knew exactly what effect an overdose would have. Dr. Evans warned her carefully enough. I could have told that fool doctor what to look for."

Shayne nodded and tugged thoughtfully at his left earlobe. "Yes, I'm sure you could, Miss Rogell. Because you put that extra teaspoonfull in his milk yourself, didn't you?"

"Nonsense. It's just that I happen to be the only one around here with a brain in my head."

Shayne shook his red head soberly. "I'm going to arrest you for poisoning your brother, Miss Rogell. And for attempting to frame Anita for your crime by putting strychnine in your own creamed chicken and feeding it to Daffy in a last-ditch effort to draw attention to your first crime."

"Of all the fantastic nonsense I ever heard!" she exclaimed crisply. "And then, I suppose, I came to the best private detective in Miami and hired him to make a case against me?"

"That's exactly what you did. After your scheme to kill Daffy fell flat on its face and she was safely buried with the strychnine inside her. It must have been quite a blow to you when these two detectives who investigated that night didn't even look into Anita's handbag and find the strychnine where you'd put it. Instead, Charles found it there, and unfortunately

jumped to the conclusion you'd hoped the detectives would reach."

Henrietta's lips were tightly compressed and she shook her gray head wonderingly from side to side. "And what possible motive would *I* have for doing all those things, Mr. Michael Shayne? You know the provisions of John's will. I'm cut off without a penny of my own. *She* gets it all." She jerked her head indignantly toward Anita. "I was the last person in the world to want to see John in his grave."

"Correction," said Shayne gravely. "You were the only person in this entire household with any motive at all. The others knew they were provided for in his will and could well afford to wait. Even Marvin Dale. Even though Rogell might have kicked him out of his soft spot here, his sister would have continued to provide for him until she came into a lot of millions on her husband's natural death. You were the only one who couldn't afford to wait for that.

"Your only chance of ever getting your hands on the money you felt was rightfully yours was to arrange it so Anita would be convicted of murdering him. In that case, the will would be set aside because a murderer cannot legally profit by her crime. If you waited for John to die normally, you were sunk. So . . . you didn't wait, Miss Rogell."

"You've got it all worked out, haven't you?" she asked sarcastically. "The one thing you can't show is opportunity. Haven't you brains enough in that red head of yours to realize that I'm the *only* person here who couldn't have dosed John's milk the night he died? All the others had a chance at it. I didn't."

"That," said Shayne heavily, "is why I suspected you from the first. The night it happened was the one night when you had a perfect alibi. That's why you weren't afraid to come to me and hire me to reopen the case. You figured you were perfectly safe. No matter who else might be suspected, it couldn't be you."

"Of all the 'Alice In Wonderland' logic I ever heard," said Henrietta with a sniff, "that takes the cake. Is that the way you solve all your cases, young man? By finding the one person who has a perfect alibi and then suspecting him?"

Shayne grinned ruefully. "It isn't always that easy. But from the beginning in this one, it looked as though you might have carefully built yourself an alibi. As though you knew what was going to happen to John that night, and provided yourself with witnesses to prove you couldn't have tampered with the chocolate milk."

"And you'll have to admit I couldn't have," she pointed out with dry satisfaction. "I was in my own room while Mrs. Blair was fixing it. She came straight up-stairs after leaving it on the dining table, and I stopped her on the way up and went up to her room with her where I stayed every minute until after he had his attack. You can ask Mrs. Blair."

"I've already asked Mrs. Blair," Shayne countered easily. "She told me the same thing . . . along with some other interesting bits of information."

He turned from Henrietta to the housekeeper who had not spoken a word since he first entered the room. "Do you remember telling me how Charles was in the kitchen that evening and poured out the last glass of milk to drink it with some cookies before you noticed it was the last and had to take it away from him so there'd be the regular cupfull for Mr. Rogell?"

"I remember that, Mr. Shayne."

"And you were surprised to discover it was the last glass in the refrigerator?" Shayne pressed on. "You'd thought there was another full bottle, but suddenly discovered there wasn't and that you *had* to have Charles' glass for Mr. Rogell? Do you remember that, too?"

"Yes, I do. I would have sworn there was another full bottle left after I made dinner."

"Did you ever stop to wonder what had become of the bottle you thought was there . . . but wasn't?"

"I don't know. I . . . I guess I didn't think too hard."

"Because you had no reason to

think about it at the time," Shayne pointed out soothingly. "You had no reason to suspect that there was going to be a lethal amount of digitalis in his milk that night, so you naturally wouldn't suspect that Henrietta had poured out the other bottle after dinner and poured digitalis into the last cup that was left . . . *knowing* that would be the cup you would put into the thermos for Rogell to drink. But now that you think back, Mrs. Blair, don't you *know* there was another bottle that disappeared from the refrigerator before you heated milk for Rogell?"

"You're putting words in her mouth," said Henrietta loudly. "No jury will ever believe her."

Shayne said grimly, "I think they will. Let's wait and see."

XII

LUCY HAMILTON had luxuriated in a long, soaking, hot bath, and rubbed soothing cold cream on her lips from which Shayne had roughly ripped away the adhesive tape. With makeup carefully applied to offset the deathly pallor of her face and arrayed in her nicest silk dressing gown and most frivolous slippers, she was happily relaxed at one end of the sofa in the security of her own apartment with Michael Shayne lounging at the other end.

She said, "I was silly, Michael. I never will forgive myself. But I

was worried about you going out to dig up that dog, and when I got the telephone call I didn't stop to think."

He said, "There was a telephone call?"

"About nine o'clock." She took a sip of her drink, then plunged into the recital with downcast eyes.

"I ate dinner alone and came back to wait for some word from you. I was sitting right here relaxing with a drink and a cigarette when the phone rang. I was so sure it would be you. I ran to the phone and a man's voice answered. He talked fast and I didn't recognize it at all. But he said: 'Miss Hamilton, Mike Shayne gave me this number to call you. He needs you fast. Meet him in his office in fifteen minutes. If he's not there, wait.'

"Then he hung up before I could ask any questions. What could I do, Michael? I was worried, and all I could think of was that the call must be from you because this number is unlisted and you're about the only one who knows it. So I called a taxi and kicked off my slippers and put on my shoes and hurried out.

"There was a car parked just beyond the office, but I didn't notice it until a man got out as I started across the sidewalk. He called to me and I turned and saw it was Charles. The block was deserted and he grabbed me and dragged me over to his car and shoved me in the front seat and stuck that adhesive over my mouth so I couldn't yell. Then he drove straight out to the house and carried me down to the boathouse and tied me up and left me. All that time he didn't say a single word, Michael. I didn't know what to think.

"It seemed like hours later when he came back. There's a telephone extension in the boathouse, and he took the tape off my mouth and made me call you and told me exactly what to say to you or else he'd kill me right off, and so I said it and then tried to tell you not to pay any attention to me, but he broke the connection.

"And then Anita's brother came stumbling into the boathouse." Her voice trembled momentarily and she paused to take a long drink. "He was obviously drunk, and Charles was enraged when he saw him. Marvin was just drunk enough to exhibit some decent instincts, and he recognized me from yesterday and wanted to know what Charles was doing with me. So Charles told him. That he was doing it all for Anita . . . to prevent you from analyzing the dog and getting an autopsy on Mr. Rogell, which he told Marvin would probably send her to the electric chair.

"Marvin didn't seem much surprised, but he drunkenly insisted that Charles had to let me go. And

Charles argued with him. He even suggested that Marvin stay out in the boathouse alone with me all night and have all the fun he wanted because, Charles told him, he would have to kill me anyhow as soon as the funeral was over and the danger to Anita was past.

"But Marvin got very angry and swore he would notify you where I was, and Charles laughed at him and said he'd never get away from the grounds and threatened to kill him, if he didn't keep his mouth shut. And they went away still arguing, and left me there, tied up and gagged for what seemed like days until you broke in the door.

"I was very glad to see you, Michael," she ended sedately, her brown eyes dancing at him over the rim of her glass as she tilted it for another long drink.

He said gruffly, "The feeling was mutual." He got out a cigarette and lit it very deliberately, stretched his long legs out in front of him and blew a streamer of blue smoke toward the ceiling.

"There's just one other question, angel," he told her in a deceptively mild voice.

"What is it?"

"You mentioned the fact that your phone is unlisted and you were thrown off-guard because only a few people know the number. How do you account for the fact that Charles knew it?"

"I was afraid you were going to

ask me that, Michael," she said in a very small voice.

He waited a long moment without looking at her. Then he said, "Well?"

"I gave it to him yesterday, Michael. When I . . . when he . . . was showing me Daffy's grave."

There was a moment of silence.

"During that 'little moment out there alone under the cypress tree with Charles' "? Shayne quoted to her from her own words yesterday afternoon.

She wet her lips nervously.

"Yes. That's when. I don't know what ever came over me."

Shayne said, "Watch it in the future when you're alone in the woods with a man and he makes you feel virginal." He put down his glass and turned to her slowly and he wasn't smiling. In a thick voice he said, "Honest to God, Lucy. . . ."

There were tears in her eyes and her swiftly indrawn breath made a little whimpering sound, and then she was in his arms, and after that no word was spoken in the apartment for a long time.

MIKE SHAYNE Presents

Next Month's Headliners

BURY ME NOT by BRETT HALLIDAY
The New Mike Shayne Novelet

PAY OFF OR DIE by RICHARD DEMING
An Exciting Novelet of the Waterfront

DEAD END by FRANK KANE
A New Johnny Liddell Story

Step Into My Parlor

*He was a sly and brutal killer.
So Ma locked the cat out and
smiled cheerfully at the postman.*

by LEE PRIESTLEY

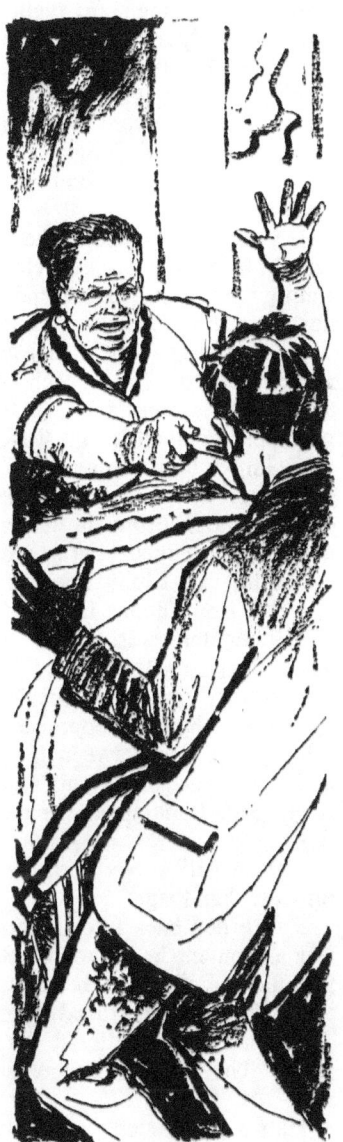

THERE'S NOTHING so hickory-rugged as an old woman. After all, what makes any muscle tough and resilient? Use and time. And an old woman's thews, both mental and physical, have been time-conditioned, time-tested.

But Johnny Mason deciding upon a hideout for the day never thought of any toughness except his own, didn't spare any attention for a female past the nubile stage. Indeed, he had never considered anyone or anything except Johnny Mason.

The suburb where Johnny had grown up hadn't recognized the corrosive ego behind his handsome face, beneath his quiet manner. So the neighborhood had been

73

stunned when one short night earlier the body of Ann, Johnny's girl friend, had been found horribly dead . . . dead of her failure to prefer Johnny over every other living thing. Now Johnny had to keep hidden until night came again.

He hadn't escaped the first search in a strict sense. He had simply ignored it. No one had supposed a murderer would cross the street from the scene of his crime and climb into a front porch glider to sleep off a murder binge. Johnny hadn't planned it that way. He had simply been sleepy.

He got into Ma Lyons' house easily enough. From the glider on the old-fashioned wrap-around porch he saw Libby Lyons come out the front door. Libby, Ma's granddaughter, was six or eight years older than Johnny and out of his orbit by reason of working in the library. Now he appraised her through the gap between the side and the back of the glider. Not really bad. If he spent the day in the house—

"Oh, blast!" Libby said, peering into her handbag.

She turned back into the house. For a moment her shadow behind the glass of the door brought out the bronze stag engraved upon it. Then her heels clattered up the stairs. The front door remained ajar.

Half a dozen steps, and Johnny was in a front parlor, dim with the blind-pulled dignity of a seldom-used room.

Ma heard Libby, too, as she clattered up and down the stairs. The careless child forgot her keys half the time, Ma thought indulgently.

"Really gone now, Ma!" Libby shouted.

The front door slammed. Ma wheeled her stout bulk down the hall to make sure the door had latched itself securely behind Libby. With such a horror happening practically on the doorstep and herself helpless in a wheel chair—

She couldn't have heard him. Certainly she didn't see him. But suddenly evil and danger were a warning taint in her nostrils. Her breath came fast and her muscles tensed. Turning her head slowly, she searched the parlor.

Nothing . . . Her eyes fastened on the folds of the velour drapes that resolutely shut out the light at the windows. Was there a bulge?

Then Johnny stepped away from the curtains, a distressed look on his face. Ma's heart leaped into her throat.

"I don't know how you got onto me," Johnny said. He casually showed her the knife in his hand. He had a gun in his pocket, too, but the knife would be quieter. "It doesn't make any difference I guess. You keep nice and quiet. Then when night comes, I'll get out. Now how about fixing me some breakfast?"

The most horrible thing about it, Ma thought, was that nothing showed. How could Johnny commit such a crime and still look human? Like any one of a thousand handsome, innocent boys? The revulsion which she felt was almost overwhelming, but she didn't let it show in her eyes. She planned quickly what she must do, how she must act.

"The police believe you are miles away by now," she said. "It's really clever of you, Johnny—to stay close like this."

She saw that she had said the right thing. Johnny looked self-satisfied. Flattery couldn't be too blatant to feed and lull that insatiable monster-ego.

Johnny waved a hand. "Cops are dumb. Well, come on, Ma. I'm hungry."

"What would you like for breakfast?" she asked. Then she half-wheeled around. "I'll open the door to air the hall. That's what I came out here to do."

If she had stopped there, it might have sounded convincing. But she heard herself going on nervously, "So much rain lately. Everything smells musty."

Johnny's face turned ugly. "Keep away from that door, Ma."

She made herself look at him. She knew that he would enjoy thinking that she was afraid of him. Fear would be a kind of admiration, a recognition of power and danger. Her hands shook as she spun the wheels to send her chair kitchenward.

Johnny was suddenly good-humored again. "Put her in high, Ma. I'm cross till I get my food. It's late for breakfast."

Ma's eyes went to the kitchen clock. This was Libby's half day at the library. In a little less than two hours she would be home again. Death for a helpless old woman would be quick, a release. But the death that lurked here for a pretty girl could be a long-drawn-out torture.

Ma wheeled up to the refrigerator. "I can give you fruit juice, bacon and eggs. If you wait a little longer I can make waffles."

"Make with the bacon and eggs."

Johnny straddled a kitchen chair. He watched Ma roll from refrigerator to stove, from toaster to pantry. "What do you need in there?" he asked.

"A jar of strawberry jam." Ma said the first thing that came into her mind.

There was no time to scan the shelves for a potential weapon. The best she could do was to drop a second jar of jam into her lap and cover it quickly with her apron. Maybe it could be used. Whatever she did had to be foolproof. She couldn't get herself killed. She had to save Libby from this smiling killer.

With the same movement that had backed her out of the pantry, she nudged the bar on Sister's door with a wheel. She pulled over the broom to cover the noise as the bar dropped.

"Awkward old fool," she muttered as she came into Johnny's view, jam jar in hand.

Sister, Ma's pampered cat, came and went as she pleased through a flap door in the outer pantry wall. Shut out, Sister invariably became indignant. If she could be kept out long enough she might mount a windowsill to stare reproachfully through the glass. If Sister chose a *kitchen* windowsill, Mrs. Chandler next door might see her. Familiar with the cat's habitual routines, Mrs. Chandler might wonder.

Ma poured orange juice and took the glass to Johnny as she placed the jam on the table. Back at the stove she lifted the bacon strips to a plate and poached the eggs with hot fat.

Keeping her eyes on the operation, she spoke to him. "Reach into that drawer beside you and get some bread for toast."

She was almost sure he would turn and do as she asked without thinking. As he swung about, she snatched the lazy tongs from their hook, beside the stove and shoved them under the blanket which covered her legs. The tongs could be extended to reach things beyond her ability, and might come in handy too. If Johnny didn't wonder how she reached the bread when she was alone.

The doorbell rang then, its old-fashioned jangle re-echoing in the hall. Ma held the plate of bacon and eggs suspended halfway between stove and table. Johnny stopped drinking orange juice in mid-swallow.

"Don't answer it," he said, choking.

"Do you want the neighbors breaking the door down to find out what has happened to me?" She gestured at her legs, useless under the blanket. "They know I haven't gone out. It's probably just the mailman."

"Go answer it, then," Johnny said. "But watch it. I'll be right behind you."

He moved into the shadows of the dining room doorway, gun in hand. Wheeling down the hall, Ma tried to plan something. Dared she risk bursting out of the door and falling down the steps? Homer Lambert, the postman, was a good boy, but a little slow. Homer would just stand there bewildered until Johnny shot him.

No one would hear the shot. Everyone worked downtown on this side of the block—except Mrs. Chandler. And she never wore her hearing aid in the morning because when the kitchen clatter was amplified it bothered her. The postman had three young children, too. She opened the door, void of any plan.

Homer stood there, letter in hand. "Good morning, Mrs. Lyons. I'll have to collect five cents on an over-weight letter, I'm afraid. I guess some young man sent too much love and kisses to Libby. Could I run back to the kitchen for you and get a nickel out of the sugar bowl? Save you the trouble?"

"No, no," Ma said hastily, aware of a faint stir in the dining room doorway. "Though it's real good of you, Homer."

She moved to the glass-topped table that displayed her cherished coin collection. "I keep a few coins here for stamps and library fines and such oddments."

She smiled brightly at Homer and added, "I just can't seem to get my library books back on time."

Maybe later Homer would notice that rare five-cent piece. Or ask himself why Ma Lyons couldn't get her books back to the library with Libby going there five and a half days a week.

"Oh, Homer, would you do me a favor?" she went on. "That book there on the hall table—"

The book in question was one of Libby's whodunits, titled appropriately, "Wanted For Murder." Johnny could see that she'd had no opportunity to sneak a message into it, since she hadn't gone near it.

"Would you take it over to Wallace Stroud, the poor man? Worried sick like he is that book is the very thing to take his mind off his troubles." She wound up hurriedly,

"And get along with you, Homer. I can't stand here all day!"

Ma shut the door firmly. Wallace Stroud, a neighbor, was the assistant district attorney. Homer might think of him as The Law. Ma acknowledged that she was clutching at a straw, but she had to try.

She was afraid to look at the clock, more afraid to look at Johnny. Johnny wasn't slow like Homer. But at least he hadn't noticed anything. He only growled with disgruntled impatience about his breakfast, now congealed on the plate. He watched her, saying nothing as she cooked more bacon and eggs.

Before he began on the second plate Johnny beckoned to her. "Roll your wheels over here, Ma. I want to keep an eye on you. I don't trust women," he added with his meaningless, flashing grin. "Not one of them. Ann, that little two-timer, sneaking out on a date with another fellow. She only got what was coming to her."

The phone started ringing then. Ma prayed harden than she had ever prayed before. Let it be Libby calling to say she would lunch downtown with the girls and go shopping.

Johnny slapped the table peevishly. "I thought old ladies led a quiet life. Go on, answer it and no funny business."

It wasn't Libby's bright voice with the lilt of laughter in it. Such bitter disappointment filled Ma's mind that it shut out comprehension.

"Hello? Hello, Mrs. Lyons?" the phone repeated. "I said, do you want anything this morning?"

"Just a minute," Ma said. "My list—" She covered the transmitter with her hand and told Johnny, "It's Sam Turner at the grocery. I call in an order twice a week and Libby picks it up on her way home."

"Okay. Give the man the order."

Maybe Johnny hadn't noticed that most grocers who took phone orders also delivered . . . Ma had spread her fingers as much as she dared. But Johnny had mouthed his words in a whisper and Sam Turner, the grocer, was growing deaf although he wouldn't admit it.

She read from the short list. "A dozen eggs. A five pound bag of sugar. Vanilla, the small size. Two packages of frozen limas and one of brocolli."

That exhausted the list. Dared she improvise?

"Sam, do you have that new corn bread mix?" she went on hurriedly. "They're advertising it on TV. Real southern type johnny cake, the commercial said. Let me think. What was that brand name? Oh, I know. 'Mason Dixon Dandy'." She overrode Sam Turner saying he'd never heard of it. "Send me a package. And that's all, thank you."

She cradled the phone and looked innocently at Johnny. It was harder to look at the clock. The hands were snipping relentlessly at the segment of time remaining. Ma tried to plan her final effort. She knew with a fatalistic certainty that it depended upon her alone. Those feeble warnings had almost surely come to naught. There was only her determination, a jar of strawberry jam and a pair of lazy tongs.

Johnny prowled restlessly from window to window now, but he kept one eye on Ma. She could conceal her racing thoughts from him but she couldn't hide the tension that was making her tremble.

But Johnny's watchfulness couldn't cope with—the sudden ringing of the front door bell, the telephone and a knock at the back door all at once. His second of startled indecision was all the opportunity Ma could have asked for, all she felt she needed. She whirled into action.

Yelling, she spun the wheel chair into a bucking charge. She slammed the jar of jam at Johnny to meet the bullet from his gun. Noise. She wanted noise now.

New to violence except on the printed page she felt a mild surprise that getting shot was no more than a stunning blow. Maybe the pain came later. She ducked under Johnny's arm. Extending the lazy tongs to the limit she wrenched the gun out of his hand. Then she clamped Johnny's handsome nose in a relentless grip.

The wheel chair pressed Johnny back against the wall. As he fought to dislodge the tongs, Ma threw herself on him, still yelling like a banshee. She clenched her gnarled hands around his throat. The weight of her heavy old body dragged him down with her as the useless legs buckled . . .

MA'S EARS picked up scraps of talk embedded in a matrix of noise and confusion. The kitchen seemed to be full of people.

"I came to bring the cat home." That was Mrs. Chandler. "I was cooking some fish and Sister simply wouldn't leave."

"Watch that broken glass," Homer Lambert, the postman, said almost in Ma's ears. "That nickel Mrs. Lyons gave me was real old and looked valuable—so I brought it back. My Lord, look at the blood!"

"Mr. Sam let me off early." The delivery boy's voice broke with his excitement. "Gosh, if I hadn't brought the groceries till afternoon, I'd have missed everything."

None of her messages had worked, Ma realized. She was being lifted now out of the mess of blood and glass, strawberry jam and splintered wheel chair. Relieved of her inert weight, Johnny Mason twitched and groaned. Ma was glad she hadn't killed him. A quick death was too easy for the likes of him.

Someone yanked Johnny urgently to his feet. "Have to put a strong guard on the jail," an unfamiliar voice said around a clicking Ma thought was handcuffs. "Treating a helpless old woman like this is enough to start a lynching party— let alone the first crime."

"Helpless!" Johnny Mason began to laugh wildly, as they led him out of the room.

MURDER IN MEXICO

An Unusual
Crime Novelet·

By
MANUEL FERNEZ

MEET Jose Pablo Enriquez
South of the border crime often wears
a garb of gaudy colors. Here's a new
and different kind of crime investigator.

THE MEXICAN SUN rose white-hot upon the town of Santiago Tlapacanas, ringed with gaunt mountains like poor relatives at the reading of a rich old uncle's will.

It frizzled the dusty leaves of the trees that garrisoned the central plaza. It belabored the cacti in the back yards of outlying houses. It nagged shabby women filling buckets at community faucets. It glared through an upper window of the Hotel Florencia to waken José Pablo Enriquez the young fiscal of Santiago Tlapacanas. Throwing aside his cotton blanket, José Pablo sat up, yawned, and flexed his lean hard biceps.

José Pablo had slept naked, as usual. His small slim torso, legs and arms were a shade less tea-brown than his straight-nosed face. From a pack on the bedside chair he fished an oval Delicado cigarette and struck a wax match.

Smoking, he drew gray socks upon his pointed feet, put on cheap shorts and tan linen trousers. He

A young Mexican lawyer must take care not to be discussed too hotly by the patrons of an ill-reputed Cantina . . . particularly when murder rears its ugly head. But José was both stubborn and courageous.

washed at the bowl on the laven-
der-stuccoed corner, shaved swiftly, and combed his gleaming black
hair. He donned a white shirt, a
narrow black string tie, a jacket
that matched the trousers, shiny
shoes with heels an inch and a half
high. He took his broad squat hat
of cream felt from the bureau-top
and went downstairs to breakfast.

In the hotel cafe an old waiter
brought him black coffee and
lightly sugared rolls. A sip and a
morsel, and José Pablo began to
consider life as he and Santiago
Tlapacanas saw and savored it.

Santiago Tlapacanas had been
a hamlet from colonial times until, in the twentieth century, the
revolutionary General Eustaquio
Guevara had caused to be set there
a court of Second Instance. After
that, the population of Santiago
Tlapacanas had grown to thirty-
five thousand, and the court was
the sovereign seat of justice for a
radius of forty miles so sun-baked-
ly unproductive that visitors called
it forgotten of God and His whole
hierarchy of saints.

There were copper mines to employ most of the seven thousand
heads of families, enigmatic *Indios*
wearing faded blue denim, coarse
hobnailed shoes and big cheap
revolvers. There were the casual
water works, the slipshod telephone company, the creaking bus
line, the third-class bull ring, the
stores, the Municipal Theatre

whose ancient curtains hung in
rags, the three or four cinemas, the
numerous and generally disrepu-
table cantinas. And there was the
Court of Second Instance, and
there was José Pablo Enriquez, the
fiscal, whose responsibility it was
to see that law was enforced and
order kept.

José Pablo was not smug about
that responsibility. It was no more
than a worthy and learned young
lawyer deserved. His poor, proud
father and mother had died while
José Pablo was at the *Universitad
Nacional*. When he had returned
with his diploma and licentiate in
law, family friends had persuasively urged José Pablo's need and talents upon the governor of the
State. They had also praised him
to Guillermo Guevara, son of the
late Revolutionary hero and by
that grace procurator-general yon-
der at the State capital.

Ay, Guillermo Guevara, the
confidently tall, the impeccably
tailored, the assuredly wealthy—
he had signed José Pablo's com-
mission. But when he visited Santiago Tlapacanas he pleasured
himself with sneering criticism and
reprimands. For Guillermo Guevara twirled his graceful mustache
at Rosalia Rivas, dweller in the
oldest and most aristocratic of the
stately aristocratic homes of Santiago Tlapacanas, she of the sweet
lemon-pale cheeks and calm bright
eyes and hair like the Night of
Affliction. Maddeningly impartial

were her smiles for José Pablo and Guillermo Guevara.

"Lamentable," babbled the waiter. "To die so young, a stranger and a heretic without hope of heaven."

"You say?" prompted José Pablo above his second cup of coffee.

"The young gringo, the guest at this hotel. You spoke to him at the dinner hour yesterday, Don José Pablo. Surely you recall that stranger in our midst."

José Pablo remembered the round American face, the new uncomfortable sports clothes, the letter from the ambassador's office in Washington *to whom it might concern*. A scholar, a writer of history, the letter had said, recommended to all Mexican officials. José Pablo had bowed and murmured hospitable banalities, then had hurried off to eat iron at Rosalia Rivas' barred window.

"And he is dead?" asked José Pablo, sipping.

"It was instantaneous," moaned the waiter with relish. "So said Dr. de Nava to Senor Morla."

José Pablo knew Dr. Franciso Javier de Nava, eighty or one hundred and twenty-five years old, stunning patients by the obscurity of his scientific language and the size of his watch. De Nava liked José Pablo, though he did not like Gonzalo Morla, the failed scientific student turned medical examiner.

"What have you told me?" José

Pablo suddenly demanded. "Dr. de Nava discussed the American's death with Senor Morla?"

"Have I not said?" asked the waiter, mopping the table. "The poor gringo died of strong poison, there in the Cantina of the Angel's Tears, on Hidalgo Street."

José Pablo sprang up so quickly that he all but overturned his chair. "Of poison?" he echoed. "Last night? And I, the fiscal, I was not informed?"

"They telephoned, Don José Pablo. But we knew, we told them that you were—importantly occupied."

Manfully José Pablo choked down a mannerless blasphemy. People at the Hotel Florencia and at the ill-reputed Cantina of the Angel's Tears had discussed, with what mockeries of tact, his visit last night to the bar-laced window in which sat Rosalia Rivas.

Hotly embarrassed, he remembered. As on so many other nights he had stood, hat prayerfully in hand, while Ceferino the *Indio* guitarist, in his abominable purple suit and grimy straw sombrero, had plucked such a muted serenade as surely would have melted the heart of a bronze statue.

Rosalia had spoken about the American cinema, of her admiration for the behavior and genius of Cary Grant and Gregory Peck. And finally, from her shadowed refuge inside: "My great-aunt Eulalia expects a call from Don Guillermo Guevara. Business brings him here tomorrow morning."

Dropping his hat, José Pablo had gripped the bars like a prisoner in a cell. He tried, as many times for three years past, to declare that his heart was at Rosalia's gracious feet. But she was saying that, since Guillermo Guevara would be a guest the following evening, perhaps José Pablo would not come to eat iron.

And long after leaving the window José Pablo had paced the plaza and the streets, demanding of himself what sins he had committed that he should be small and poor while Guillermo was upstanding and rich to gain the favor of Rosalia's great-aunt Eulalia and entry to that aristocratic old house while he, younger and truer of heart, could approach no closer to the bars on the window. . .

"The tragedy must be investigated," José Pablo told the waiter bleakly. "I will telephone Senor Morla and Chief Baños. The Cantina of the Angel's Tears, you said?"

"On Hidalgo Street," said the waiter again, and gestured. "But a few steps around the corner."

ANY ANGEL OF reason and breeding would have wept for the reputation and decor of the Cantina of the Angel's Tears. It was a broad low cave of a place, with a zinc-topped bar against a wall that bore shelves of bottles. By night it was evilly illuminated by three or four small electric bulbs, daubed over with red paint to emit a glow that sensitive habitues likened to coals on the floor of hell. Even by the hot morning light through open door and raised windows, it looked like a proper setting for sordid, tragic, and appallingly violent death.

At the bar, Dr. de Nava drank morning tequila and talked to Otero, the globular white-shirted proprietor. A languid retainer mopped the floor with carbolic-laced water, the sharp smell wrestling with a century's stale cigarette smoke. Against the rear wall. Ceferino squatted on the heels of his fantastically ill-kept two-toned oxfords, his precious old guitar cuddled between his knees, as he munched fiery-sauced tortillas.

"This murder—" began José Pablo without ceremony as he hurried in.

"It was no murder," wheezed de Nava, dabbing salt in the fork of his thumb. "The American came to me because of his diseased heart. I gave him strychnine pills." From the doctor's beard-spiked mouth crept a lean shrivelled tongue to lick salt before another gulp of tequila.

"I was here," ventured Ceferino. taking another tortilla. His free hand evoked a jangling whisper from the guitar strings. "I saw him fall."

"Then he was murdered," José

Pablo pounced upon this declaraion."

"So says Senor Morla," qualified Otero, without great interest. "My friends, what would you wish? A man's clock strikes at a certain moment, his life ceases." His lardy shoulders shrugged philosophically. "Who am I to oppose the decree of heaven?"

Dr. de Nava trickled more tequila into his glass. In his lapel drooped the faded ribbon of the Order of Guadalupe, fourth class. "You may say what you wish, for the laws of the State and the Republic give you freedom," he halfsnarled, "but experts, not laymen, establish whether death came by chance or by evil design."

"True," nodded Otero agreeably, "and Senor Morla says—"

"Morla, who could not pass his medical examinations!" exploded Dr. de Nava. "Who was rejected with scorn when he sought to become a doctor!"

"By your favor," said a voice from the door, "when an unfortunate one comes to my official notice, he is past need of doctors. That should be self-evident."

In strutted Medical Examiner Gonzalo Morla, like a natty, derisive brown cricket. In his wake trundled the khaki massiveness of Police Chief Baños. The chief's uniform swelled with heaped muscles. His copper-tray face wore a great thicket of mustache, accentuating a natural resemblance to

the late Pancho Villa. Low at his broad leather belt rode a mighty holstered revolver.

"We are here at your orders." He smiled fearsomely at José Pablo.

"I was about to begin the autopsy when you telephoned," added Morla.

"Where did you learn of autopsy?" sneered Dr. de Nava. "At the municipal slaughterhouse?"

Morla opened his mouth to reply witheringly, but José Pablo halted the words with a gesture. "Ceferino, you said that you were here last night. You came when you left me?"

Ceferino swallowed a last bite of tortilla, filled with beans and pepper, and rose, skinny inside the immemorially wrinkled purple suit. His dark hand's heel rubbed the wood of the guitar.

"Many came here," he said. "I sang, old songs and those of my own devising, and the customers were generous." He patted a pocket. "The American was happy in his drink—much tequila. He paid me to sing *La Cucaracha,* and begged his friend to teach him the words that he might sing with me."

"What friend?" asked José Pablo.

"Unknown to me," said Ceferino.

"And to me," seconded Otero. "Neither young nor old, as I judge. Of middle height, perhaps. His clothes were old, his shoulders bowed thus." He illustrated with a sag of his own soft bulk.

"A horseman," elaborated Ceferino. "His legs were bent by the saddle."

"His face?" prodded José Pablo.

"His mustache pointed downward," said Otero, sketching on his own fat face with a finger. "His eyes shone like stars under his hat."

"He did not take off his hat?" inquired Chief Baños.

"The question!" cried Otero scornfully. "Am I a priest, that men should take off their hats to me?"

"That stranger murdered the gringo," said Morla.

"But they were friends," argued Otero. "The stranger showed the gringo how to drink tequila. Himself he put salt on the gringo's thumb, himself he sliced the lemon to suck."

"And when the gringo fell," added Ceferino, "the friend cried out: "He is sick Fetch a doctor!"

"Those were his words," nodded Otero. "We put the gringo flat on his back. His face was dark, he made himself turn and twist like a worm."

"Strychnine," diagnosed Morla, crinkling his nose at de Nava.

"The other ran out, crying for a doctor," went on Otero. "I send Ceferino for Dr. de Nava. And I," he touched his thumb to his chest," "telephoned Senor Morla."

"The poor American was dead when I arrived," said de Nava, his veined old hand cradling the tequila bottle. "Too many of my pills."

"Then it is you who poisoned him," snickered Morla.

De Nava drew up his withered herring of a body. "He came yesterday, complaining of his heart. The pills from my dispensary had each but the thirtieth part of a grain of strychnine—a small proportion to give health to a laboring heart, not death."

"The fourth part of a grain will kill," said Morla. "Ten such pills as you gave him, Doctor, would do his business. Professional negligence."

"What when the dead one was taken away?" José Pablo asked Otero.

"I told the customers that the matter was in the hands of our able officials," said the proprietor, and, at the expense of the Cantina, served a round of drinks."

"Of the cheapest," elaborated Ceferino to his guitar.

"Senores, the American's government will make inquiries," said José Pablo. "Dr. de Nava, you opine that it was an accident. Perhaps suicide?"

"But the gringo was happy," argued Otero. "His heart was glad with drink and music and hospitality."

"My autopsy will decide the question," insisted Morla.

"And then begins the search for this stranger, if he is the murderer," grumbled Chief Baños. "He must be taken to the capital for trial."

"Senores," spoke up Ceferino suddenly, "search no further. I poisoned the gringo."

They all looked at him. His hand swept the guitar's strings.

"Have I not said he interrupted my singing, tried to sing with me?" he demanded rhetorically. "It was more than I could bear."

Baños shot out a broad brown hand to seize the front of Ceferino's purple coat. "You confess this, *hombre?*"

"Have a care for my guitar," squealed Ceferino. "There is no need for these wrestlings."

Baños' other hand prowled inside Ceferino's coat and brought out a revolver almost as big as his own and fully as well kept. It was one of perhaps five thousand revolvers owned and habitually carried by Santiago Tlapacanos, but Baños shook it triumphantly at José Pablo, then at Morla, and stuck it into his own waistband.

"Are strangers to be murdered for nothing in our town?" he scolded Ceferino.

"You do not understand the heart of a musician," flung back Ceferino. "Let me go. I said I poisoned him, I will not run or hide."

José Pablo shook off his stunned amazement as a dog shakes off water. "This is a mad joke, Ceferino," he protested.

"It is the truth, Don José Pablo," Ceferino assured him above the imprisoning fist of Baños.

"And no joke," added Baños. "Come, you. It remains for this confession to be written out and signed. Are you able to sign your name, assassin?"

He hustled Ceferino out at the door. With one hand Ceferino clutched his straw sombrero, with the other he held his guitar out of danger's way.

Morla twinkled spitefully at Dr. de Nava. "Murder," he gloated. "I said so from the first."

"For what trifles an *Indio* will kill," contributed Otero, in whose own fat-swaddled veins flowed blood perhaps seven-eighths of the *Indio* strain.

"Senores, what of the other doctor who came?" José Pablo found time to wonder. "The doctor brought by the American's friend."

"His friend?" echoed Otero. "But his friend did not come back."

"His testimony will not be needed," added Morla. "My autopsy will prove—"

"Delay the autopsy," José Pablo bade the medical examiner, "until we read the confession of Ceferino when it has been reduced to writing. I will rely upon you, Senor Morla, and you, Dr. de Nava, for your own signed statements. Shall we say an hour from now, in my office at the city hall?" He started for the door. "At present, I must examine the belongings of this deceased one."

JOSE PABLO'S KEY opened the door of the American's room, as it would have opened the door to any other room of the Hotel Florencia. Inside, José Pablo made a thoughtful search, jotting notes on a sheet of hotel stationery. When he had done, his list included the following:

Various garments and shoes, of good make and material but amusingly inappropriate for Santiago Tlapacanas and its rugged environs.

A large suitcase and one not so large, of gleaming plastic.

An electric razor, a toothbrush, a soap dish and a bottle of scented shaving lotion.

A tourist card issued to Wilbur Waldorf Mayberry—maiden name of mother, Jenkins. It said that Wilbur Waldorf Mayberry was a student by profession, twenty-eight years old, single, Protestant, and a resident of Kansas City, Missouri, U. S. A.

A folder of travellers' checks to the amount of $325 American.

The Spanish-American Frontier Historical Association Quarterly for the previous winter, including in the table of contents on its cover an article entitled *New Light on a Revolutionary Struggle*.

A box full of big brown pellets, with a label proclaiming them to be vitamin pills.

A vial containing eighteen pills of an unappetizing pinkish purple, with an attached sticker bearing, in Dr. de Nava's spidery handwriting, the name *W. W. Maiberri* and a cabalistic prescription number.

A carton of American cigarettes, trumpeting in capital letters its boast of utter supremacy in the filtering away of all deadly characteristics tobacco might contain.

A ballpoint fountain pen, its tiny golden point exposed as though ready to write.

José Pablo, proficient in English, first studied the guide book. The marked passages nearly all concerned hotel rates or locations of libraries. Then he took up the magazine, and saw that the struggle on which new light proposed to shed itself was the savagely brilliant campaign of General Guevara's Revolutionary troops in the Santiago Tlapacanas region.

The author was one Alvin A. Hurwitz, professor of Latin-American history at Missouri University, who had little information not familiar to any literate Santiago Tlapacano. But José Pablo felt a quiver of pride in his town's history as he read one paragraph: *An epic might be written of how this peasant column scored a series of victories over superior forces. Arming and feeding themselves from the captured camps of their ad-*

versaries, they then marched for a sudden stroke at the flank of a larger army and a greater victory, which resulted in gratifying new seizures of stores, including money to settle six months' arrears of pay.

A footnote flew up to catch José Pablo's eye: *The researches of Mr. W. W. Mayberry toward his forthcoming doctor's dissertation may supply many details of Guevara's encouraging and, as it proved, decisive success.*

The poor dead gringo, reflected José Pablo, to find so horrible and violent a fate in the town whose history he had hoped to write. Regrettable, tragic. But, had he lived —more published praise of General Eustaquio Guevara, reflecting its glow upon his son Guillermo, impressing Rosalia Rivas. José Pablo left the room, locked the door and made for the city hall.

The pavement along the plaza teamed with citizens of high degree and low. At the corner opposite the city hall paused a group of four. At the sight of one face, José Pablo's heart kindled to adoring fire, at the sight of another his liver gushed bile.

Rosalia stood with her great-aunt and a broad-bodied maid who held two market baskets. Before her towered the maddening elegance of Procurator-General Guillermo Guevara, his expensive American hat in his hand, studying charm into the upward twirling of his mustache. Dye in that mus-

tache, snarled José Pablo in his jealous heart, and in the hair that receded from the brow to give it a special appearance of intellectuality.

It was all elaborate fraud.

Rosalia's great-aunt, gaunt and deaf, cupped a hand at her ear to catch Guevara's pleasantries, and laughed. Rosalia lowered her lids —demurely or provocatively?

As José Pablo approached, Guevara fixed him with a condescending eye.

"I have just arrived," he announced, "and was on my way to your office. What is this rumor of violence to the American tourist named Mayberry?"

"He was murdered," said José Pablo, bowing to Rosalia and her great-aunt.

"Murdered?" barked Guevara. "But he wrote that he would meet me."

Grimly respectful, José Pablo told of Mayberry's death and Ceferino's confession.

"Infamous!" snorted Guevara. "How do you perform your duty in Santiago Tlapacanas, Senor Fiscal, that such things befall guests, distinguished foreigners? I await a sensible reply."

A tamale peddler lagged to listen. José Pablo waved him away.

"The murderer is now in my office," said José Pablo, sad in his heart for that excellent guitarist Ceferino.

"What gutter-scouring is this

confessed murderer?" demanded Guevara, then bowed to the ladies. "Your gracious pardon that these vulgar matters should be told before you, but I have my duty to the State. Nothing must be allowed to interfere with that."

Rosalia's sweet voice repeated into her great-aunt's ear what Guevara and José Pablo were saying.

"Senor Fiscal," said Guevara, "this matter touches me personally. I drove swiftly this morning, seventy miles from the capital, in response to a letter from Senor Mayberry. Hear what he says."

From inside his jacket he brought an envelope and slid a folded sheet from it. He began to read, in a voice harsh enough to be understood by Great-aunt Eulalia:

" 'I am grateful for your generous offers to help my studies. It was my good fortune recently to secure a series of letters written by your illustrious father to J. J. Phelps, a St. Louis banker, at the time of the Santiago Tlapacanas campaign. These may be interestingly new even to you, his son, and together we should find in them the importances my dissertation would employ."

Guevara put the letter away. "Other matters in his communication are of a personal nature. But you can see that I feel as though I had lost a friend, though I knew Senor Mayberry only by correspondence."

"We understand," murmured Rosalia, as though in awe.

"Forgive me if I am delayed in my call at your gracious home," Guevara overwhelmed her, bowing again. "Senorita Rosalia, Senora, until soon. Senor Fiscal, you will accompany me to your office."

Crossing the street to the city hall, Guevara spoke disparagingly of Santiago Tlapacanas' residents and cantinas. He mentioned the more decorous cantinas of the State capital and their less violent clientele.

"I am persuaded that there should be an investigation of the lawlessness permitted here," he grumbled as José Pablo opened the door to his office.

Inside, the walls were heavily plastered, like the outside walls of a house. There were a battered desk, a telephone, filing cabinets and two chairs. There were also Ceferino, Baños, Otero, Dr. de Nava, Morla and Baños' best-educated policeman. This man sat at the desk, writing in a loose-leaf notebook. Dr. de Nava had the other chair. Ceferino squatted against a wall with his guitar, and Baños stooped menacingly above him.

"Is that the culprit?" demanded Guevara as he entered. "Why is he permitted to sit while he is questioned?"

Rising, Ceferino bobbed his head respectfully. "Senor, I have thrice told how I murdered the gringo."

"Each time differently," complained Baños. "Assassin, tell us, on peril of your soul, where you got the poison."

"I have said that a Chinese sold it to me," Ceferino replied patiently. "What reason would I have to lie to you about such a thing?"

José Pablo checked a handful of articles on the desk—a wallet, two or three crumpled bills, a watch, a handkerchief, a spectacle case.

"The contents of the American's pockets," the policeman told him.

"Ceferino," said José Pablo, "you say you were enraged because the American tried to sing with you."

"I could endure his bleating no longer," agreed Ceferino. "I became as a madman, thirsting for his blood."

"A killer by natural instinct," put in Baños. "See, Senor Procurator-General, he carried this revolver."

He drew the weapon from his waistband. Quickly José Pablo put out his own hand to take it.

"Ceferino," said José Pablo, "why did you not shoot the American with this?"

Ceferino shrugged above his guitar. "I was too angry to think. The gringo infuriated me. It must be as Senor Baños says—my instinct led me."

"Your instinct led you to poison the American?" inquired José

Pablo. "Ceferino, you are more subtle than I knew, who have hired your music many nights. You carry a revolver and a dose of poison, and your instinct prompts you to the poison before the revolver."

"I did not care for his life or mine," insisted Ceferino doggedly.

"But you ran to fetch Dr. de Nava," pursued José Pablo.

"That is so," agreed the doctor's weary voice. "Ceferino pleaded that I hurry and save a poor tortured stranger."

"Do not wag your beard, old man," Guevara snubbed the doctor.

"Senor Fiscal," spoke up Baños, "you speak wisely. As Senor Otero remarked at the cantina, *Indios* are swift to kill. And I have always found that pistols come most readily to their hands."

"Silence, you also!" snapped Guevara. "I congratulate myself that I am here to procure this guilty one's confession, what with the incompetence of local officials." He towered over Ceferino. "You try to play the jester with us; then I shall dictate a statement of your crime, and you will sign your name, if you have so much education."

"By your favor, Senor Procurator-General," said José Pablo suddenly. "Ceferino, is not the State capitol thrice the size of Santiago Tlapacanas?"

Ceferino looked blank. "But we all know that, Don José Pablo."

"The Procurator-General spoke

as we came here," continued José Pablo, "of the many cantinas at the State capital, and of their superiority to ours. In such cantinas, a musician would find listeners more generous and more appreciative than here. Have you not thought that, Ceferino?"

Ceferino grimaced. "You speak things a simple man does not understand," he pleaded.

"And no Mexican court will convict an innocent man, especially if he says he was crazy when he confessed," summed up José Pablo, as to a jury. "Such an unfortunate one, set free, might even have fame in the newspaper accounts. He could look for applause and full pockets in the cantinas."

"*Huy!*" boomed Baños. "Have you thought, Ceferino, to make sport of honest officers?" He took a step toward Ceferino, who sidled close to the door.

José Pablo pointed the revolver. "Stir a toe from here," he warned Ceferino, "and my bullet will smash your guitar."

Guevara found his voice. "What fantasies are these?" he roared. "The man said he was guilty."

"Only to get a free ride to the State capital," said Baños, brightly informative.

"An artist is always misunderstood," Ceferino reproached them all.

Otero and Morla began to chatter. Dr. de Nava started toward the door. "I have thirst," he said.

"Remain, you old fool!" commanded Guevara. "Chief Baños, are you and the fiscal in a conspiracy to defeat justice? I must see to this murderer's indictment and trial. You two shall suffer as well, for malfeasance in office."

"But Ceferino is not guilty," Baños half-pleaded.

"Then who"

"You are guilty, Senor Procurator-General," accused José Pablo.

Guevara widened his eyes. José Pablo could see the whites all around the irises. Then Guevara's mustached lips cracked into the bitterest grin ever seen in Santiago Tlapacanas.

"Senor Fiscal," he said measuringly, "you throw away your career for the sake of an insane joke."

"Senor Procurator-General, I never spoke more sanely and gravely in my life."

"I killed the American?" whooped Guevara. "But I did not leave the capital until this morning, driving swiftly!"

"Swift driving could have brought you here last night, and more swift driving taken you back before dawn," replied José Pablo. "With time between to telephone the man who endangered you, take him to that dim cantina, and there kill him."

"There is meat in these words," contributed Dr. de Nava, his old hand tweaking his gray beard-point.

"You made much of reading me

his letter, to convince that you had not come before this morning," said José Pablo evenly. "But it helped point to you. It spoke of other letters, from your father to an American banker. Those letters vanished. They were not in his room, nor are they with his things there on the desk."

"Next you will say that I took the letters!" spluttered Guevara.

"Next I will say even that. The American was a scholar, a writer of history—but no written word could be found in his room. Ceferino would not have taken his writings. There have been many jokes about Ceferino's signing of his own name."

"I can write," volunteered Ceferino, "if someone holds my hand with the pen."

"Why should my father not write to an American banker?" argued Guevara. "Senor Mayberry would not have asked my help on something that would damage my father's character."

"He did not know, Senor Mayberry did not know," replied José Pablo. "To him the letters were but history, not personal matters. But men write to bankers about money. Now, there was a magazine in the American's room you did not think worth taking along with the letters."

"A magazine—"

"I read in it of how your father defeated and plundered one enemy force, but had to defeat and plun-der another before he could pay his men from the money chests of the second vanquished enemy." José Pablo gestured triumphantly with the hand that did not hold the revolver. "I suggest that your father kept for himself the money from the first capture, and sent it to the American bank to found his own fortune."

"My honored father is dead," said Guevara tightly, "and cannot defend himself against your cowardly slander. Yet if it were true —and you are mad to say that it is—even your trifling legal sense assures you that I cannot be held responsible for such a matter."

"The captured moneys belonged by right to the Revolution," returned José Pablo. "The government, hearing about them, would ask for their restoration by you and your father's other descendants, who would be nothing without money."

"José Pablo speaks with reason," commented Morla.

"His summation is impressive," nodded Dr. de Nava, forgetting that he agreed with Morla for the first time in their association.

Chief Baños sidled close to Guevara, who glared at them all.

"You suppose that I poisoned Senor Mayberry," he exploded frantically. "Who saw me in the Cantina of the Angel's Tears?"

"Ceferino saw you," said José Pablo helpfully, "and Senor Otero."

Otero giggled and shook his head, but Ceferino jumped up.

"There is truth in that," he assured José Pablo. "I thought his legs were bowed by riding, but—"

"And he humped his shoulders," added José Pablo. "that he might appear short. He wore his hat low, and the dimness cloaked him."

"All I saw of his face was dangling mustaches," remembered Otero.

José Pablo pointed the revolver at Guevara. "Do not move," he warned, and stepped close. With his free hand he dragged down one tip, then the other, of Guevara's mustache.

"It is he" cried Otero.

"And he dabbed strychnine on the American's thumb, instead of salt for his tequila," summed up José Pablo.

Guevara snatched at Ceferino's revolver in José Pablo's hand. At once Chief Baños caught Guevara's shoulder and whirled him violently away and into a corner.

"Hands to yourself, murderer!" he bawled.

"Chief Baños, I will see you discharged," promised Guevara, with cold fury.

"You have already threatened that," Baños reminded him. "We await your confession."

"I confess nothing."

Baños' mighty paw clamped the procurator-general's beautifully tailored arm. "My office is at the other end of the hall," he announced, with a slow, greedy smile. "We will discuss your confession, you and I."

"Not one word will I say to you," Guevara assured him.

"I expect eloquence of you, when we are alone together in the back room." Baños tugged powerfully. "Come."

They departed. The policeman with the notebook followed them. José Pablo took the telephone from his desk and asked the operator to connect him with the governor at the capital. He tapped the desk-top impatiently while he waited.

For a full minute José Pablo listened to noises as of jangling tin plates. Then came the voice of a secretary in the distant city, the voice of another official, finally the voice of the governor himself, faint but recognizable.

"José Pablo Enriquez, Excellency. The fiscal at Santiago Tlapacanas."

"Why do you telephone, Senor Enriquez?"

"Murder has been done here," said José Pablo. "An American, Wilbur Waldorf Mayberry."

The governor repeated the name. "I think he was commended to me by our ambassador. Murdered, you say? Who murdered him?"

José Pablo moistened his lips. "It was the procurator-general, Excellency. Senor Guillermo Guevara."

"Nonsense, Senor Enriquez!

Mockery, libel—what do you mean?"

Quickly José explained about the poison, the missing letters, the other evidence against Guevara. As he spoke, the door burst open and in tramped Baños, flailing his thick arms.

"He is a suicide!" Baños panted.

"The poor gringo?" asked Morla.

"No, no, the procurator-general. He swallowed a pill." Baños himself swallowed in embarrassment. "Not a question had I asked, not even a blow had I struck. He swallowed it, he fell and wriggled—thus, like a fish. His face turned dark blue."

"*Ca!*" cried de Nava. "Strychnine again!"

"Surely an autopsy is called for this time," said Morla briskly. "Dr. de Nava, if you will give me the benefit of your observation."

Happily the two followed Baños out. Otero waddled after them. Only Ceferino remained with José Pablo, his thumb plucking a guitar string.

"Excellency," said José Pablo into the telephone, "Senor Guevara has killed himself, with the same poison that killed Senor Mayberry."

Silence inside the instrument. At last: "Ah!" crooned the governor's voice. "And you feel that this establishes his guilt."

"I must feel so, Excellency."

Another pause. far off there at the end of the wire. "I, too, must feel so. Senor Enriquez, for many months I have noticed your conduct in office. The State now finds itself without a procurator-general."

"Yes. Even now they begin an autopsy on Senor Guevara's body."

"Consider yourself temporarily appointed to the post of procurator-general," the governor's voice commanded.

"I!" bleated José Pablo.

"Temporarily," repeated the governor. "Permanence may depend on the intelligence and comprehensiveness of the report you bring me. The written result of the autopsy, the statements of the witnesses, the Revolutionary money. all such things. How soon will you present yourself?"

"A bus leaves for the capital in the morning," said José Pablo. "It should arrive by noon."

"At noon, then, I expect you. Make your report justify your permanent assignment. It might please the American officials if the man who solved their countryman's murder is rewarded by promotion. Until tomorrow, Senor Enriquez."

NIGHT FELL UPON Santiago Tlapacanas, as abruptly as black coffee from an overturned cup. José Pablo stood at the jail-like bars of Rosalia's window. Five paces away, Ceferino touched tactful chords on his guitar.

"José Pablo," said Rosalia from

the darkness inside, her voice as soft as the voice of a sinner's conscience.

"You have heard all things?" he asked her.

"About Don Guillermo?" He guessed, rather than saw, the twitch of her lovely shadowy shoulders. "I am a woman, I do not presume to understand legal matters. Yet, if he killed himself in the same way that the gringo was killed—"

She left the sentence for José Pablo to finish. While Ceferino wove with delicate fingerings the melodious fabric of a tear-summoning song called *The Cup of Sorrow,* José Pablo finished it.

"The governor agrees that he was guilty. I am summoned to be procurator-general in his place."

"Imagine!" she breathed, very close to the bars.

José Pablo felt the utter appropriateness of that idiom about eating iron. He could have crunched those bars in his teeth like candy.

"I must leave for the capital tomorrow," he said, almost in doleful time to Ceferino's music. "The governor's order requires me there, far from this town of my birth." He saw the brightness of Rosalia's eyes in the gloom. "Far from my friends, my acquaintances," he mourned.

"The capital is a center of intellectuality," she observed. "And of polite manners."

"I will be lonely there," José Pablo dared to quaver.

"Because you are single, José Pablo," said Rosalia. "A forsaken and solitary man without a family. Had you a wife—"

Again she left him to finish what she had begun. This time he dared not. Ceferino's brown fingers tweaked tearful minors.

"Your man plays well," said Rosalia. "I have heard that you too play the guitar—"

He stood dry-mouthed, unable yet again to fill out her sentence.

"The gardener left the gate unlatched, careless as he is," Rosalia told him. "Should you enter quietly, I could bring out the guitar."

"But—" José Pablo was stammering. "You and I alone!"

"It will be proper, my great-aunt is here," she said.

"What happened to Don Guillermo prostrated her. She is confined to her bed—at the front of the second floor." Rosalia gestured, in the opposite direction from where the garden lay. "And her hearing, poor dear one, she could barely hear if it thundered."

Her skirts rustled as she rose. "The gate is unlatched," she said again.

José Pablo ran to Ceferino, thrusting money at him. "Drink my health," he commanded. "Swiftly, at once—as soon as you can get to the Cantina of the Angel's Tears."

Ceferino trotted away. With trembling hands, José Pablo fumbled at the catch of Rosalia's garden gate.

A
Perfect
Crime

by JOHN ROWLAND

The crime sparkled. But so does a flawed diamond.

FEW PROFESSIONAL criminals ever achieve what they consider to be a perfect crime. For an amateur criminal to achieve it is almost unique. Yet Mr. Josiah Flower thought that he saw a way to pull off a crime magnificent in its conception and wonderful in its results.

Mr. Flower had been for nearly twenty years in the employ of the

United Ebony Company. Starting as an office boy at 15 shillings a week, he had managed to work himself up to general secretary of the company, at a salary of 750 pounds a year. Some of his subordinates in the general office considered that "Old Flower"—actually he was just over forty—was one of the worst slave-drivers in the City of London, and a man, moreover, who did his work with a nasty zest in order to earn some fabulous salary.

Josiah Flower, in actual fact, thought that the directors were the real slave-drivers, pushing him around in order that they might get out of him more cash than they put into his pocket.

He knew that he would have been cheap at fifteen hundred pounds a year. But he continued to work at a miserable seven hundred and fifty because he was out to create an impression, and because he felt tolerably sure that at the end of a further two or three years he would be able to get away with a large sum.

What helped to make him tolerably sure was the fact that, once every six months, large sums of cash were handled in the office of the United Ebony Company. It had some expert agents who operated in some African colonies, buying the wood that was the main article in which the company dealt. These buyers were not fraudulent, but many of the things

which they did could not be wisely paid for by check. Indeed, many of the overseas buyers insisted that they should be paid in cash.

On June 30 and December 30 each year, therefore, a large sum of money lay in the safe of the United Ebony Company, and to get this money from the bank was one of Mr. Josiah Flower's regular jobs. He would leave the office, go around the corner to the London and County Bank, and come back with a bag containing some thousands of pounds in pound notes.

It was one of Mr. Flower's perpetual gripes against the firm that he carried in that bag, each June 30 and December 30, a sum of money which was equal to several years' salary for himself.

He made up his mind that before too long that large sum of money would be his. That this would mean disappearing, and that as a result he would sacrifice his 750 pounds a year, did not worry him unduly. After all, most people would prefer to have 5000 pounds in cash rather than the right to earn 750 a year for the next ten or fifteen years.

On that particular June 30 Mr. Flower did his usual task. He went to the City branch of the London and County Bank, and drew out 5122 pounds, 17 shillings and 8 pence. The odd silver and copper was for stamps. Then he hailed a taxi. Thus for the first time he went slightly adrift from his usual habit.

MR. JOSHIA FLOWER was a tall, thin man with a greying mustache and hair that had already turned almost white. During recent months various people at the office had remarked that Mr. Flower was aging. His stoop was getting more pronounced, and his mustache and hair were getting whiter. Although only about forty, he began to look nearer sixty.

His colleagues did not guess that he was simulating a stoop, and that his hair and mustache had been treated with a special compound which bleached them without giving them that peroxide color so disliked by most people with some taste.

Mr. Flower was a bachelor. He could keep things to himself. Especially could he keep to himself the fact that the bottle of bleaching compound now lay at the bottom of the Thames, and that in his pocket was a bottle of a guaranteed fast dye, which would turn his mustache and hair a glossy black in a matter of minutes.

When he came out of the bank and called the taxi, he asked to be driven to Waterloo. There he paid off the taxi-man, and made his way to the cloakroom, where he collected a small suitcase, left there earlier in the day. With the suitcase, he went to the station's main lavatory, where he locked himself in.

He rapidly discarded his brown suit, even removing his tasteful brown and white polka-dot tie. Then he put on a blue serge suit with a blue tie to match. This done, he took a little of the dye, and rubbed it carefully into his hair and his mustache.

All this had taken merely ten minutes. But it had changed a stooping man in late middle-age, a man dressed in brown, to a young man dressed in blue serge.

Mr. Flower emerged from Waterloo Station, and hailed a taxi in Waterloo Road. He instructed the driver to take him to St. Pancras. There he bought two tickets—first-class return to Bedford and third-class single to Leeds. There was no harm, he told himself, in confusing the issue a little, in case the police did get on his track. But Mr. Flower was fairly certain that he had, in recent months, established his new identity, and that there was no chance of the police catching up on him.

By this time there was, of course, a hue-and-cry in the City. It was thought that Mr. Josiah Flower, that trusted servant of the company, had been waylaid and robbed. And that, of course, was just what Mr. Flower wanted people to think. The longer they continued to think it the happier he would be, for the colder the trail would become.

He got into a long-distance train, bound from St. Pancras to Bedford. Meanwhile, he had thrown the return half of his Bedford ticket on the line, where it might, or might not, be recovered.

As the train swung over a bridge, the muddy water of a canal twinkling beneath, he threw the suitcase with his other clothes in it out of the window. He had, of course, weighted it before. Mr. Flower was a thorough man. The London-Bedford ticket he flung out as the train slowed down outside Bedford Station.

In a few hours he was alighting at Leeds, there to make his way to the bus station and to board a bus for Ilkley. The conductor recognised him. "Good evening, Mr. Weenen," he said. "Not often you're here, barring week-ends?"

Josiah smiled. "I'll be here a bit more now than I've been able to be in the past," he said.

"Brought off a good deal, eh?" the conductor said with a grin. "Plenty of brass, eh?"

Mr. Flower smiled. "I wouldn't say plenty," he remarked. "But I should say enough to be getting on with."

And so Mr. William Weenen, who had been a frequent week-end visitor to a pleasant little private hotel at Ilkley, now became a more or less permanent visitor there. He settled down and made friends, he paid his way, and now and then he paid a little cash into the account that he had started at the Yorkshire Bank some months earlier.

No one knew just what he did. There was a little gossip now and then, when he went wandering off on the moors by himself. But apart from his unusual desire to see all the London daily papers every morning, there was nothing very striking about Mr. Weenen.

And Josiah Flower was glad to see that his exploits in London, which had first been headline news on the front page, gradually became small paragraph stuff on an inside page, and then disappeared altogether.

He had first felt a little nervous when pictures of himself appeared, but he blessed the foresight which had made him get a studio portrait done, with his white hair and his pronounced stoop. Nobody connected the lively young man at Ilkley with the elderly gentleman who had disappeared in London.

Mr. Flower congratulated himself as summer passed into autumn and autumn into winter. It was all right, he told himself; he had got away with it.

It was the perfect crime. No one suspected him. The clever part of his scheme had been the building up of a new personality in Ilkley *before* committing the crime.

Gradually he became part of the social life of Ilkley. He was invited out, more and more, to social functions of one sort or another. He became quite a good bridge player, and in the hotel he won the snooker handicap and the darts championship. Young Weenen became popular, in a way in which Old Flower never had been. Mr. Flower congratulated himself on his skill.

He even succeeded in making friends with the local Superintendent of Police, who was a warden at the church which Mr. Flower thought it good policy to attend. Superintendent Jenkinson often came around to Mr. Weenen's hotel for a game of cards.

After six months of life at Ilkley Josiah Flower was almost forgotten. It was only in the privacy of his own room that Mr. Flower permitted himself the luxury of remembering his own name. Mr. Weenen was such a friendly soul that no one gave him a moment's thought.

Josiah had worked out a good signature for William Weenen. It was a big, elaborate affair, which finished off with a flourish. It was quite unlike Josiah Flower's signature, which had been small and neat.

Josiah in his guise of William Weenen had often talked about crime to Superintendent Jenkinson. The Superintendent assured him that the police never forgot a crime.

"There are no such things as unsolved crimes, William," the Superintendent would say. "There are only crimes which have been put back in the pigeon-hole for the moment. But they'll come out again."

And Willaim Weenen, who was Josiah Flower, perpetrator of the perfect crime, would outwardly agree.

"I've got in my office," the Superintendent once said, "a list of wanted people, a list of those who've disappeared, and a list of those we would like to see but don't expect to."

"You keep the list up to date?" asked Josiah.

"Yes. Now and then someone is caught, and then I cross a name off the list. Now and then someone gets away with another crime, and I add 'em to it. But the list always stays there, and I study it from time to time, to make sure that I'm not forgetting any of them."

After that conversation it was some little time before Josiah Flower felt comfortable with Superintendent Jenkinson. But then one day the Superintendent called around. "The vicar has asked me to make a little collection," he said.

"Yes?" said Mr. Weenen.

"Yes," said the Superintendent. "Mr. Harrison, the organist, is leaving, and they want to have a little presentation to him. The vicar asked me to sound out a few of the congregation. Would you care to give something?"

"Delighted," said Mr. Flower. This was the first time he had felt at all comfortable with the Superintendent since his previous very awkward conversation with that gentleman of the law. He was sure now that the Superintendent had no suspicions connecting William Weenen with Josiah Flower.

"I'll be delighted to give a guinea," he said, getting out his check book and writing the check. He folded it in two, and handed it to the Superintendent.

"Thank you," said the Superintendent, and left.

It was ten o'clock that night and Mr. Weenen was having his last whisky and soda in the bar, when the Superintendent returned.

"Could I have a word with you in private?" his visitor asked.

Josiah looked at him curiously, but said nothing, merely leading the way to the lounge. "Now what is it?" he asked.

"Are you prepared to make a statement?" said the Superintendent.

"A statement? What about?"

Jenkinson smiled grimly. "About a certain five thousand pounds, *Mr. Flower*," he remarked.

"I . . . I . . . I don't understand."

"Oh, yes, you do," the Superintendent said, holding up a check —the check which Josiah had drawn some two or three hours before. It was signed *Josiah Flower*.

Three SHAYNE *Stories*

You May Have Missed

If you've just discovered our magazine you may not have read any of them. And if you are a real dyed-in-the-wool Shayne fan—and who isn't?—you'll want to read them. We have a limited supply left and they are yours—by sending in for them immediately.

1 copy @ 35c   2 copies @ 70c   3 copies @ $1

No. 1 . . . DIAMONDS FOR A LADY
The longest Shayne we've ever printed—it is full-length and cost $2.95 when it came out in book form.

No. 2 . . . TOO DEAD FOR THE MONEY
The girl had a vital natural grace—but a man had been murdered. Mike had to earn his fee the hard way.

No. 3 . . . WITNESS FOR THE DECEASED
It's hard to get at the crucial facts when you are cross-examining a corpse. Mike had to use his wits.

PREVENTIVE MURDER

by C. B. GILFORD

A sound knowledge of modern psychology could probably prevent a good many murders. But when a man or woman commits a major crime . . . that particular remedy doesn't carry much weight.

HE WANTED A GUN. He desperately wanted a gun. If he'd had one in his hand, or if there'd been one anywhere within reach, he would have used it. He would have aimed it straight at his brother's smiling, mocking face, and he would have pulled the trigger. Then he would have had the pleasure—the infinite pleasure—of seeing how a bullet hole punched into that hated image could erase the smile on it forever.

And then later he himself would have been dragged off to execution from a death cell, helplessly screaming the truth, "He didn't deserve to live!"

But he was saved from destroying the face and thereby destroying himself by the fact that there was no gun. There was only the vase of flowers sitting there on the little table. "Damn you, Rex! Damn you," he said, and he picked up the vase and threw it.

His aim was fairly good, but his brother ducked easily, and the vase smashed into a hundred fragments against the wall.

"Allan boy," Rex said, still smiling and without resentment, "I'm ashamed of you. Throwing a vase is a woman's trick. If you're crazy enough to think you're defending your honor or your girl why don't you act like a man? You know damned well I'll fight you if you care to fight."

His fury was so intense that he might have accepted the challenge. He might have rushed blindly at his tormentor, his fists flailing. There was Rex standing before him, the smile on his handsome face now a maddening grin, relaxed, lazy-looking, his hands at his sides.

But he didn't make that blind, futile rush. Because at the last second he realized the futility of it—realized that a fight with bare fists was just what Rex wanted. Rex would win a fist fight. In the last twenty years there must have been a hundred such fights between them. And Rex had won all of them.

So they were still standing there confronting each other when Jim the houseboy came in. Jim must have heard the sound of the vase crashing against the wall. He hesitated in the doorway, impeccable in his white shirt and black bow tie, his dark oriental face carefully expressionless. His eyes flicked immediately from the now empty table to the debris on the floor.

"Vase fell off the table," Rex explained casually. "Pick it up, will you, Jim?"

"Sure, Mister Rex," the boy said. He turned and vanished quickly to get his dustpan and broom.

"Allan," Rex said, "you're making the servant problem very tough. We're lucky to have a boy like Jim. But he won't stick with us if he has to keep cleaning up after your infantile tantrums."

Allen was seething with frustration, but he had only words to fight back with. "You go to hell," he said. And then to hide the tears that came burning to his eyes, he turned away and rushed into his bedroom, slamming the door behind him.

For long minutes he lay on the bed, staring at the ceiling, and thought about his life.

It had all started with his mother really. Allan had never known his father except from photographs, because his mother had become a widow when Allan was less than a year old. Rex was five then, a handsome young animal already, and bearing a remarkable resemblance to the man in those photographs. It was probably only natural for a bereaved woman to be partial to the son who was the image of her dead husband. More proud of him and more attached to him than to the son with the nondescript appearance, a plain-faced throwback to some previous generation.

Thus it was that Rex, with the curly hair and the flashing dark eyes, with four years seniority in age and size that his younger brother never made up, got the best of everything right from the beginning. The best toys, the best schools, and finally when Mother died, the lion's share of the family inheritance.

And out of it all, somewhere along the line, Rex had acquired a habit too. A nasty, vicious little habit that didn't operate all the time—just on special occasions.

At other periods, Rex could be a prince of a guy, but now and then circumstances arose which never failed to bring out the beast in him. That was whenever Allan got something that was very precious and valuable to him. Then Rex would be seized with an insane desire to smash it, destroy it utterly. And he always succeeded.

At first toys. Sometimes even an old toy that Rex had discarded and Allan had rescued from oblivion. Allan would develop an attachment for the thing, and Rex would notice it. Then deliberately —oh, so deliberately and maliciously—he would break it beyond all repair. The tragedy would be heightened and made more bitter by Allan's fury, the inevitable fight, and the inevitable victory for Rex. And finally, afterward, a slow forgetting and forgiving—in childhood at least.

Later on it was the things of school. A favorite book, a modest but dearly cherished athletic trophy. The fights became more bitter, more bloody, and hopeless. And the forgetting and forgiving increasingly harder.

That had been the pattern of their lives, until Rex's departure for the university had separated them for four years. Later, while Allan attended the same university, Rex had launched his business career. Finally Mother's death, and Rex getting all the money and Allan being forced to come and live with his brother in his nice apartment, the poor relative on a small allowance.

Almost immediately the old pattern had begun to repeat itself. Not with childhood things any more, nor with the things of adolescence. Now at last they were practically of the same age. They were young men together. And the major interests of young men are women.

"Oh, Shar," he muttered aloud. "Shar, how could you do it? I loved you so much."

Then he thought of the gun again. What would he have done, he wondered, if there had been a gun? Would he really have used it? Yes . . . yes, he would have. He'd lost all control for a moment. It was the old rage, stronger now that he was a man. The anger had cooled now just a little, enough for him to examine it. Yes, he would have killed his brother over a desperately desired woman.

But the woman was finished now, broken as those old toys had been broken. He had always forgotten the toys, at least eventually. Would he forget Shar? And finally, with the passage of time, would he be able to forgive Rex?

There could be only one answer. He would have killed Rex when rage had filled his whole being, but the pattern of eventual forgiveness was too strong to be broken.

If it could have ended there,

then perhaps the loss of Shar was a tragedy he could learn to live with. But he knew this wouldn't be the end of it, for Rex hadn't changed. Rex still liked to smash and ruin everything that was precious to his younger brother. So it would be certain to happen again. He would have the desire to kill Rex again. And some day he *would* kill him.

I'm going to kill Rex, he thought. Somehow, sometime. I'm going to kill him.

He got up from the bed, lit a cigarette, and stared out of the window. No, he thought, I don't have to commit murder. I can simply pack up and leave. I can forget I have a brother. If Rex and I never see each other again . . .

His lips tightened in bitterness. It wasn't that easy. As he always had before, he might forgive and forget again. And come back. And besides, running away would leave Rex with all of his mother's money, the luxuriously furnished apartment, an oriental houseboy, all the good things of life. Rex with everything and himself with nothing. Because he, Allan, was a coward.

But the alternative was murder. As certain as the rising of the sun, or his own eventual death. He would acquire something new and precious, Rex would destroy it, and in his fury he'd want revenge.

It's going to happen, he thought. I'll kill him in a fit of

anger, and I'll go to prison for the rest of my life unless . . . unless first I kill him in a different way. Premeditated, planned, safe . . .

The cigarette burned his fingers before he remembered that he still held it. Quickly he ground it into an ashtray. But he was too preoccupied to do anything for the burn. He continued to stare out of the window . . .

HE WAS PUTTING his idea into operation when he went to see Shar. He didn't tell Rex he was going to see her. In fact, he hadn't seen too much of Rex in the past two days. Rex was pretty busy. Not with Shar, but with some business deal he was keeping silent about. In his characteristic way, Rex seemed to have forgotten Shar, forgotten the argument, forgotten everything. He behaved toward his brother as if nothing at all had happened. And Allan was content to let things ride along that way.

It was reassuring to know that when he went to see Shar, he wouldn't find Rex there. It was a Saturday, so he was pretty sure she'd be home. He took a taxi to her apartment, rode up in the elevator, knocked briskly at her door.

She seemed surprised to see him. Perhaps, he told himself, she'd expected Rex to be standing there. Or possibly she'd guessed by this time that Rex wouldn't be back any more. But even if he was

right in his second surmise, it was an obvious shock to her to see Allan. She just stood there for a long minute and stared at him in tight-lipped silence.

"Yes, it's me," he said, at last.

She looked as if she'd been crying. Her eyes were dry now, but they were swollen and drained of all animation. No longer sparkling and brilliant blue. Her lips and the rest of her face were without make-up, and there was a certain unkemptness about her blonde hair. She was still pretty, of course, but she was changed. Very changed.

"May I come in?" he asked.

She opened the door wider to let him enter. Then she walked ahead of him into the living room. He watched her without desire. There was a listlessness in her walk. She was wearing a robe, not a specially new or attractive one, as if she hadn't really been expecting anyone.

They sat down opposite each other—she on the sofa, he on the big hassock. She didn't look at him, and they were both silent for a moment.

"What do you want, Allan?" she asked him finally.

He felt sorry for her. He was very sure it was nothing more than pity. He had never really considered her predicament before. But now that he did consider it, he realized that she had been a victim, nothing more. A pawn in the ancient game between him and Rex.

"I wanted to see you again," he said. His pity lent genuineness to his tone.

"Why should you? Don't you know . . . ?"

"Oh yes, I know. Rex isn't one to keep a secret of that kind."

Her hands were tense and white in her lap. "I'm sorry, Allan," she began.

"You mean you're sorry you did it?"

She shook her head. "No, not exactly that. I suppose I'd do the same thing over again if I had the chance."

"Yes, Rex is a fascinating guy to women, I suppose."

"What I'm really sorry about, Allan, is that I hurt you. I didn't want to hurt you. I just couldn't help it, that's all."

"I know that, Shar. I know you couldn't help it. Nor could I. Tell me something. Do you love him?"

"I don't know. I don't know whether I ever loved him really. It wasn't a question of love."

How right she was, he thought grimly. No, it hadn't been a question of love. At least not on Rex's side. He had simply made callous, calculating use of her.

"It's very strange," she went on. "I think I knew all the time. I was aware of what he was doing. Some instinct warned me that he really didn't want me, that all he was

trying to do was make a conquest. And I let him."

Yes, he was sorry for her. Her helplessness and frustration were so like his own had been.

"I loathe myself," she said. "I feel unclean. I'm a horrible person, Allan. I hate myself especially because, as I've said, I'd probably let him do the same thing all over again. And that's strange, because I had no real love for him. What's wrong with me?"

She didn't seem really to expect an answer. He had the answer, but how could he explain it to her? How could he explain to her that Rex had wanted her only to triumph over his younger brother. He could not be cruel enough to tell her that. She had suffered enough already. She didn't yet realize the full extent of the disaster. Some day she would understand that Rex had used her, that he had never had the least affection for her, much less love. Some day she'd understand that she loved Rex, despite her denial now . . . and what would she do with herself then?

Suddenly he felt his fury rising again. Rex had cruelly injured this girl, not just physically and for the moment, but forever.

He forced himself to remain calm. He was going to kill Rex. But he must do it coolly, carefully, safely. The one thing in the world he wasn't going to do for Rex was allow himself to be punished for murdering him.

"What do you want, Allan?" she was asking again. "What do you want from me?"

He lied. It was necessary for him to lie, vital to his plan. "I came to tell you I still love you, Shar," he said.

It startled her. She looked at him directly for the first time.

"I mean it, Shar," he said. "I don't care about the past. Rex doesn't want to marry you. I still do."

"No, Allan . . ."

"Oh yes, darling. I'm going into this with my eyes wide open."

"But I don't love you."

"I know that. But I still love you. A good marriage doesn't always have to start with a deeply shared love."

She turned away again. "I don't know what to say, Allan. I'm so confused."

He crossed to the sofa and sat down beside her. Gently he put an arm around her shoulders. She didn't resist him. "You don't have to decide right away, darling," he told her. "I'm patient. I can wait . . ."

While he was waiting, he made his other preparations. He went to see Shar every two or three days, but he didn't press her for a decision. He simply kept her steadfastly assured of his love, so she'd be ready to use when the proper time came.

The key to his plan was the bottle of champagne. He bought it the day following his first visit to her apartment. It was an expensive bottle of champagne—a very good year—a purchase he could ill afford. But he had to have it. He bought it and hid it in his bedroom.

The next articles he needed were the long hypodermic needle and the poison. The needle was easy enough to secure. But he had to put thought and research into his selection of the poison. It had to be relatively tasteless, quick-acting—and most of all, absolutely fatal. It did not matter whether evidence of it could be detected later, and it did not matter whether his purchase of the stuff could be traced.

He decided finally upon two poisons—one containing aconite, the other arsenic. The two drugs, he felt, would make the outcome all the more certain. After all, the most urgent necessity was that Rex should become ill and die before any medical aid could be summoned.

And that, of course, must be accomplished not in the heat of passion when mistakes can occur, but calmly, coldly, when there could be no possibility of a mistake.

He had all the components of his plan ready now, and he ticked them off: the champagne, the poisons, the needle. And his actors were ready too. They all had a place, a function. Shar, Jim, and of course, himself.

He made certain of Shar first. When he went to see her on that fateful Tuesday night, he had his approach well-rehearsed.

Her emotional state hadn't improved much in the past two weeks. In fact, it had apparently deteriorated a bit further. She'd let herself go, and even for a pretty girl like Shar, such physical carelessness took its toll. And in addition there was an increasingly tragic and hopeless emptiness inside her, leaving her listless, her eyes vacant, her thoughts wandering and far away.

"Shar," he began as soon as he arrived, "I think we should get engaged right away."

Her eyelids fluttered at him in a helpless way, like the waving hands of a drowning man. "But, Allan, you know . . ." she started to say.

"Shar, listen to me. Perhaps we can strike a kind of bargain. If things work out as I hope they will, we could get married real soon. We could go away, somewhere far off. I'm convinced you could forget about Rex eventually. If not, we could write it all off as a mistake. I wouldn't complain. I'd have had my chance at least. Don't you think you owe me that much, Shar—a chance?"

She hesitated, her hands twisting in her lap, her eyes frightened. "There's another way it could

work out, of course," he added shrewdly.

She took the bait. "What way, Allan?"

'Well, if by any chance Rex loves you—or could come to love you—this would give him the necessary prod. You know how jealousy can wake a man up."

It was obvious that she liked the idea, that she was aware by this time that she loved Rex, and that she thought the opportunity was worth taking.

"We might do it this way," he went on quickly. "A little engagement dinner at my apartment. I'll mention it to Rex. That'll give him his chance to take you away from me if he wants to."

Her eyes were wide with fear now. But a desperate hope kept her voice steady. "You mean I'd have to see Rex again?" she asked.

"Let's put it this way," he corrected her. "Rex would see you again."

She pondered for a long moment. The conflict inside her was clear to him. But he knew already what her decision would be.

"All right," she said.

A thrill of exultation went through him. He looked at Shar, impervious to the mingling of terror in her eyes. He could think of only one thing. She was serving his purpose. The trap was laid . . .

HE HAD CHOSEN a night when Rex had said he'd be going out.

"A dinner here?" Jim the house-boy echoed.

"That's right, Jim," he repeated. "An engagement dinner for Charlotte Fennelly and me. All the trimmings, Jim. Something real fancy to eat, candlelight, the best silver, music, soft lights. You know, Jim, the works."

"Miss Fennelly?" Jim asked uneasily.

"Sure, Jim. We'll have this dinner. Then I'll ask the question. With all the right atmosphere, I know she'll say yes."

But Jim was disturbed. That, of course, was strictly what Allan had been counting on. Jim knew the score, all right. Jim had good ears. He'd heard the angry conversation with Rex a fortnight earlier. He'd heard Rex say what he'd done to Shar. And he'd swept up the pieces of the broken vase. And now here was Allan saying he was going to get engaged to the girl. Jim was confused. The oriental face was properly inscrutable, but Allan knew what the houseboy was thinking.

And he knew also—which was the important thing—what Jim would testify later.

The afternoon before the dinner party he completed the mechanical part of the operation. He worked inside his locked bedroom. He brought out the champagne and his other equipment from their hiding places. He went through all the necessary motions with a deadly outward calm that was surprising, considering the inner excitement which was making his temples pound. His hands were patient, steady.

The syringe sucked the twin poisons out of their little bottles with gratifying efficiency. Then without the least trouble, the needle penetrated the wax seal on the champagne, glided slowly and easily down through the deep cork. Stopping to peer inside the dark bottle, he saw the point of the needle extended well below the bottom of the cork. Exerting pressure on the plunger with his thumb, careful not to snap the needle, he watched with satisfaction as the fatal drops splashed down to merge with the wine. Drop by drop, till the syringe was empty.

When he withdrew the needle finally there was only a tiny hole in the wax seal, which a little careful massaging passably obliterated. He was quite sure that an unsuspicious person, opening the bottle, would not notice it. The corkscrew would take care of any visible hole in the cork. He jiggled the bottle a little, to make certain the foreign ingredients would thoroughly dissolve in the champagne.

Then he washed the syringe, returned everything to its place of concealment, and started to get dressed. When he'd finished that task he checked with Jim.

The houseboy was doing his job well. The small dining table was already covered with a snowy cloth. There were fresh flowers on it, a pair of candles, silver that was freshly polished and gleaming. Jim was at the stove in the kitchen.

Allan went back and fetched the champagne. Then he called the boy. Jim came out of the kitchen, cool and immaculate as the table itself in his short white jacket.

"Jim, I'll want this iced," Allan said, showing the bottle and setting it on the table. "Most expensive stuff I could find. But nothing's too good for the girl I'm going to marry, isn't that right, Jim?"

The boy's face smiled woodenly, properly. He still didn't understand, or maybe he didn't approve this tolerant attitude of the western world. But he was getting the point, that was the important thing. *The champagne was intended for Shar.*

"Yes, sir," Jim said, and returned to the kitchen to obey instructions.

A few minutes later Allan heard Rex's key in the hall door. A moment passed, and then the door swung open, and Rex strode in. He saw Allan and the table almost immediately. He was plainly surprised and curious. Jim hadn't told him about this dinner. Allan had counted on that. He had been almost sure the houseboy would keep a circumspect silence.

"What's this?" Rex wanted to know, coming closer. "Im not eating at home tonight."

Allan fought down his mounting excitement. This was the most difficult part of the plan, and it had to be handled just right. Coolly, dispassionately. Whatever Rex says, don't lose your temper.

"I knew you were going out tonight, Rex. That's why I took the liberty . . ."

Now his brother was really interested. "This isn't for us then, Allan boy?"

"No, not exactly."

Neither of them was trying to speak softly. That, too, was part of the plan. It was important that Jim, lurking in the kitchen, should overhear this conversation.

"You're having a guest for dinner?"

"That's right."

"Well, come on, don't make me ask a million questions. Who is it?"

"Shar."

It was obviously not the answer that Rex had expected. "Shar!" he repeated. Then he smiled. "Are you kidding, Allan boy?"

"No, I'm not kidding. In fact, it's a kind of celebration. An engagement dinner."

Again the surprise on Rex's good-looking face. Not the surprise of pain or shock though, but rather of amusement. "You're getting engaged to Shar?"

"Yes," Allan said.

"You mean you're going to marry her?"

"Yes."

"Even after . . .?"

"That's right, Rex. Even after everything."

"Allan boy, you're a glutton for punishment—self-imposed."

They faced each other for a silent moment. Allan was sure he could read his brother's mind. Rex had broken and spoiled everything that was terribly precious to Allan. He'd thought he'd taken Shar away from him by a calculated act of betrayal. Well, maybe he hadn't completely succeeded after all. And maybe Shar was more precious to this younger brother of his than he'd imagined. Here was a challenge. What was to be done about it? Well, Allan had just the opportunity ready for him. And Rex's eyes were darting over the table and the preparations, as if searching for that opportunity.

This was the moment, the climactic moment. "Well maybe," Allan began, with careful, deliberate hesitation, "maybe I've overstated the case a little. I haven't actually given Shar an engagement ring. But I've seen her a few times, and she has consented to come to dinner tonight. And she knows the purpose of this dinner. So I thought maybe with the proper atmosphere and everything . . . I could cheer her up a bit, could make her see this thing my way.

"You see, I've forgiven her, Rex. I've forgiven you too. You didn't really care about her. It was just one of those things you seem to have a compulsion to do. Well, you've done it now. You've had your fun. And it's all over. I think Shar and I can patch things up, and make a good life together."

"Wait a minute," Rex said, "Let me get this straight. There's no hard feelings?"

"No hard feelings, Rex. Oh, there could be easily enough. But I really love Shar, you understand. I'm not going to let anything stand in the way."

"You think you can bring her here, and get real romantic?"

"You don't mind my using the apartment, do you, Rex?"

"Oh, no, it isn't that, Allan boy."

"I thought I could tell just how much she means to me better here than in some public place. We'll be completely alone here. After things get underway, I'm going to get rid of Jim. And you'll be gone too, of course. There'll be the candlelight. And this champagne. The champagne is the key to everything, really. People always feel elated, you know, when they're drinking champagne. Painful or tragic memories recede, fall away . . . ."

Suddenly Rex was laughing. His teeth were flashing white in his dark, tanned face Allan knew that he was laughing at his, Allan's, desperate, sad little attempt to be a big man, to emulate a man of the world's techniques . . . and at the certain futility of it all.

Rex could hardly stop laughing, but he managed to say, "I'll leave in about half an hour, Allan boy."

Allan left the bottle of champagne on the table and went to the door, picking up his hat on the way. Behind him he heard another laugh and Rex calling after him, "Good luck, Allan boy." Then he was safely outside in the corridor.

He checked his time, took the elevator downstairs, and hailed a cab. The ride to Shar's place was only a matter of minutes. Then he was there, knocking at her door, the excitement inside him harder than ever to control.

When she answered his knock and let him in, he was startled by the change in her. There was make-up on her face now, and brightness in her eyes. She was wearing an evening dress, dark blue, frilly, and her shoulders gleamed white above it. At another time she would have seemed charming, tremendously appealing. But he felt not the slightest tremor of the old desire. She was a tool to be used, nothing more.

"Will Rex be there?" she asked quickly, unable to repress or conceal her real interest.

"I told him you were coming," he answered truthfully. "He was there when I left. Whether he'll stay or not is up to him."

Her hands fluttered to her bare throat, to her cheeks, to her carmined mouth. "Let me look at myself again," she said. "I won't be a minute."

He watched her go into the bedroom. He had a little time to kill. Rex had said half an hour, and Jim surely had heard him say it. So he didn't want to return too soon.

He lit a cigarette to give his hands something to do, and sat down. This might be the very moment, he was thinking. It might be happening right now.

"Allan boy," Rex would say when they returned, "I knew you'd want me to drink your health, and Shar's health. But I also knew you two would want to be alone. So I thought I'd have my drink first, before you came back. And you know, the damn stuff was so good, I finished the bottle, Allan boy."

But then he, Allan boy, would go into his act. Shock first, confusion, delay, until he was completely sure the swiftly working aconite was already beginning to do its job. Rex would be in pain. A doctor would have to be summoned—Jim's task. And Jim would be slow with it. More time for the doctor to arrive. Then Allan's halting explanation that Rex had swallowed not one poison but two—two poisons to make the doctor's task more hopeless. Well, there wouldn't be any doubt of the outcome by then.

And finally the police. This was the really masterful part of the plan. No complicated concealing of his trail to worry about. No attempt to hide the identity of the poisoner—who always had to be one of very few possible suspects. "The champagne was intended for Miss Fennelly, don't you see? Ask Jim. Yes, I was going to kill her, because she had betrayed me. And kill myself with her. That is, unless she promised to marry me tonight. It was an engagement dinner, you see. But if she'd promised to marry me, I never would have killed her, or killed myself either. And I don't think I'd have let her drink the champagne anyway. I doubt if I could ever actually commit a cold-blooded murder. But the poison certainly was never intended for my brother. That was an accident."

An accident. An accident that was Rex's fault alone. Not murder. Not legal murder. And not murder in the unguarded moment of passion . . .

When Shar emerged from the bedroom he became suddenly and uncontrollably impatient. He wanted to get back to the apartment fast, in case the timetable should have somehow speeded up. "Let's go," he said, taking firm hold of Shar's arm.

The return ride in the taxi seemed eternally long. There was no conversation between them. Both their minds were contemplating what they would discover at the end of the ride.

Finally, at long long last, their destination, and the silent ride up in the elevator. Allan used his key to open the apartment door, pushed Shar in ahead of him. Then they saw Rex.

He was standing beside the candle-lighted table, a sneering smile on his face. The bottle of champagne was nowhere in sight. There was a long silence.

Allan was only vaguely aware of Shar, on the periphery of his vision, white-faced, terrified. He was only aware of the awful pounding of the blood in his veins, and the expression on Rex's face, malicious, triumphant. He's dying right now, Allan thought. I've won, and in just a moment . . .

"About that bottle of champagne, Allan boy," Rex began finally.

"What about it?" Allen scarcely recognized his own voice, so altered was it.

"Come here a minute, Allan boy."

He obeyed, walking slowly, hypnotized by Rex's face, searching the features for the first sign of pain. Then somehow, as he got to the table, the direction of his gaze followed Rex's floorward stare.

(Concluded on page 122)

It was a very rich fruit cake, with currants and a lemon peel to enhance its flavor. So naturally the dash of arsenic was a great shock—almost an affront—to Inspector West.

A Piece of Cake

by JOHN CREASEY

CHIEF INSPECTOR 'Handsome' West of the Yard looked into the pale, frightened face of the woman who had accompanied him into the tiny, spotless kitchen, and wondered what secret fears tormented her.

"It's so awful, the doctor says that he might die," she said. "Why, it's terrible. We've been married nearly twenty years, and—and—" She drew in her breath, as if in physical pain, and then went on in a broken voice: "And to think he should die through eating a piece of the cake I made for him!"

She burst into tears.

Without trying to soothe her, West stepped to the table where Detective Sergeant Bell of the Criminal Investigation Department was looking at a piece of rich, dark fruit cake.

"I suppose the arsenic was in this," Bell said. He was a big, fair, florid man, deliberate and slow-moving, an excellent foil to West, who did everything briskly.

The Chief Inspector moved, spoke and even looked about him as if he was a jump ahead of everyone else, but would not dream of saying so. He was as tall as Bell, a spare, lean man.

116

"No shadow of doubt about the poison," he said crisply. "The analyst's report on the contents of Harold Rawson's stomach proves that conclusively. Actually, white arsenic was found inside pieces of currants, sultanas and lemon peel, and not just where you would expect to find it—in the general mixture. The bitterness of the lemon peel probably concealed the flavor of the arsenic."

"And Mrs. Rawson made the cake," Bell mused. "Wonder if she has a boy friend waiting to step into her husband's shoes. These middle-aged women who manage to keep their figures almost girlish at forty often go off the rails."

"You go and pick up what local gossip you can while I see if there's anything I can do here."

West looked compassionately at Mrs. Rawson, who had stopped crying. He knew exactly what Bell meant about her. She was extremely attractive and girlishly slender, and he found himself admiring the way she appeared to be fighting back her grief.

"Mrs. Rawson, I want to make this as easy for you as I can," he said quietly, "but you know that we must do everything we can to find out the truth, don't you?"

"I know you must, but I didn't—" Mrs. Rawson broke off, and screwed up her eyes; and West could just barely hear her next whispered words. "They'll all say I did, though. They'll all say I poisoned him."

"You mean the neighbors?"

"Yes, everyone."

"Why should anyone accuse you?" West inquired.

"They—they know Harold and I weren't getting on too well," Mrs. Rawson told him, and either she was almost naively honest, or very, very clever. "It isn't really my fault, though. You see, I came

into some money a year or two ago, and ever since then Harold has been telling everyone he hates being a rich woman's husband—I'm not really rich, of course. But he can't bear the thought that I have more money than he has." Mrs. Rawson broke off again, and then declared very firmly: "But I don't care what anyone says. I didn't put any poison in that cake."

"How much of the cake did you eat yourself?" asked West.

"Oh, I never eat rich fruit cake," Mrs. Rawson told him promptly. "It doesn't agree with me."

It hadn't exactly agreed with her husband, either West thought dryly. He tried another approach.

"Who else was here when you made it, Mrs. Rawson?"

"No one at all," she assured him. "My husband and I are quite alone. Both my children have gone abroad to live, you see. One's in Canada, the other—"

West interrupted this almost eager statement, which, ironically enough, weighed the scales even more heavily against Mrs. Rawson. He could almost hear prosecuting counsel rubbing his hands over that tidy bit of freely volunteered information.

"Don't you ever have friends in?" he asked. "For cards, or a cup of tea?"

"I haven't had anyone in even briefly for weeks," said Mrs. Rawson. "I went out that very morning and bought all the ingredients, and made the cake that same afternoon. Why, the baking smell was so rich that Harold actually complimented me on it! It isn't often that he says anything really complimentary these days."

She seemed unwittingly intent on self-destruction.

"Thank you," West said dryly. "Now I want you to answer me very carefully," he went on in a sharper tone. "I want you pay careful attention to every word you say in reply. Do you understand me?"

She looked at him as if she was really seeing him for the first time. His keen grey eyes were at once challenging and commanding, but he eased the tension by smiling just a little. Most women were impressed by his good looks, even when they pretended not to be. Mrs. Rawson seemed to take no notice of them at all.

"Are you quite sure no one else was here when you made that cake?" demanded West.

"I wouldn't think of lying to you about it," said Mrs. Rawson, almost hotly. "I took it out with my own hands, too. I was extremely careful, but the gas pressure's so unreliable these days. I don't like a cake of mine to split at the top, but except for that it was perfectly cooked, even if I do say so myself. And to think—"

West interrupted again, hoping that his brusqueness would make her realize how important her answers were.

"Did anything unusual happen that evening, Mrs. Rawson?"

Mrs. Rawson's face took on a new expression. It was unmistakably an expression of dismay. Here was the first crack, West thought. She was no longer answering spontaneously, but beginning to think of the consequences of what she was saying.

"Well, no, not really unusual. Mr. Lee popped in to ask if he could borrow some tea, that's all, and I told him to help himself. Harold had gone out for a beer, and I was looking at television. There was nothing to it, honestly."

Now she was protesting too much; and even when thinking of what she was saying, she made the circumstances look damning.

"Is that quite all?" West asked coldly.

"Well, Mr. Lee and I may have flirted a bit, but it has never been serious," Mrs. Rawson said huskily. "Only—only Harold saw Mr. Lee give me a kiss when he left, and there were a few angry words exchanged."

That was the moment when full realization of what she was doing dawned on her, and she caught her breath.

"Had you turned the cake out by then?" West asked.

"Oh, no! I always leave a rich cake in the tin all night. You see, if you turn it out while it's hot it'll break to pieces in your hands."

Bell came back in time to hear that, and West went with him into the living-room, leaving Mrs. Rawson in the kitchen with her old and her new fears.

"Not much doubt how this is working out," Bell said in his earnest way. "Mrs. Rawson's been carrying on, as they say, with a neighbor named Lee who lives across the landing."

"She told me something about that," West said.

"Oh, she'll brazen it out," Bell said, "but she hasn't a chance. She made the cake, she baked it, and all the ingredients were fresh from the grocer's that day. She's been on bad terms with her husband for years, and much too friendly with a good looking bachelor neighbor. Are you going to charge her right away, Handsome?"

"I'm going to have the rest of this cake analyzed," West said. "I want to know whether the arsenic is spread all about the cake, or only in one spot."

"I see," Bell said. "Nothing like being thorough, especially when it's a woman you're after. If her husband dies it'll be a murder rap, and even if he comes through it'll mean several years for attempted homicide. Juries get sentimental if you give them half a chance."

"We'll just give 'em all the evidence we can find," said West dryly.

"Supposing the arsenic is only in one spot, what will that tell you?" Bell asked.

"Good question," West said. He grinned and fell silent.

For the rest of that day Bell avoided him. A thoughtful, stubborn man, he did not like to think he had missed any significant item of evidence.

Yet he was in the laboratory, early next morning, when West heard the analyst's final report. The remainder of the cake was on a large plate, beautifully browned, its only blemish the crack which had been an insult to Mrs. Rawson's baking.

The analyst, a dry-voiced, impersonal man, pointed to a broken slice of the cake, and said briskly: "There's enough arsenic in that slice to kill a dozen men, Handsome. It's inside the currants and raisins, too. In fact, it couldn't be more thoroughly mixed up in that section. Only—"

"None in the rest of the cake?" Bell burst out.

"Why don't you apply for a job in this department?" the analyst asked sarcastically. "You wouldn't need to do a chemical analysis— you'd just have to smell the answer. No—none anywhere else. Not a trace."

"That's what I hoped—" West began, but Bell interrupted him, almost aggressively.

"Well, some of the filthy stuff was in the slice that Rawson ate.

He was bound to get a poisoned piece sooner or later, as Mrs. Rawson doesn't eat rich fruit cake."

"What's on your mind, Handsome?" the analyst asked.

"For some reason he doesn't want to pin this on Mrs. Rawson," Bell said, fighting to keep indignation out of his voice.

"Ever helped your wife in the kitchen, Bill?" West asked him, mildly.

"I'm the Force's champion dryer-upper, but I don't see—"

"Did you ever test a rich fruit cake, to see if it was properly cooked?"

"Dozens of times. You stick in a long hat pin or a thin piece of wire, or—"

"A thin-bladed knife," West finished for him. "The chief puzzle in this job was how the arsenic got inside the fruit of the cake, not just in the mixture. You won't deny that. Mrs. Rawson could have done it, of course. But would anyone in her position break open currants and raisins, put arsenic inside, and then repeat the process a dozen times when she could have sprinkled the poison all through the mixture. It's unthinkable. There'd be no point at all in doing it so carefully in this case. Since the victim was going to eat the entire cake eventually, no particular slice mattered. Agree about that?"

"I guess I'll have to," Bell said.

"We also know that only one person could have mixed arsenic in the entire cake," West went on. "But someone beside that opportunity-favored person could have put it in one particular spot."

"You mean the boy friend, Lee, when he came to borrow the tea and have a kiss and a cuddle," Bell scoffed. "Tell me how he or anyone else could put arsenic inside the fruit inside a baked cake, all surrounded with greaseproof paper, and inside a tin. She didn't turn it out till morning, remember."

"It could be done this way," West said, still mildly. He picked up a thin-bladed knife, and smeared it with a paste gum from a bottle on the analyst's desk. "See the cake, Bill? See how it's cracked on top? The oven was too hot when she first put it in, although she blames it on to gas pressure. Anyhow—put a clean, sharp, thick-bladed knife into a cake fresh from the oven, and make a kind of channel in the cake by working the knife to and fro. The knife, going in, would cut through some of the fruit, although whoever did it wouldn't be likely to think of that.

Withdraw this knife, and push into the channel a thin-bladed knife, coated with arsenic. Like this gum, for instance. The arsenic would go inside the individual pieces of fruit, wouldn't it? And when the knife was withdrawn, the heat of the cake would gradually close the channel—and in the fruit. The poisoner had some luck-too, because of the crack in the cake. He didn't have to leave a noticeable blemish on the surface. That's how it was done, Bill, and that's why I'm going to see neighbor Lee."

"You mean, Mrs. Rawson didn't know?" Bill Bell asked in a squeaky voice.

"I'm pretty sure she didn't," West said. "I think we'll find that Lee could smell the cake baking. There's an open fanlight at the passage door, and we know that the smell was pretty strong. Lee probably wanted to marry Mrs. Rawson for her money—the cause of her trouble with her husband—

and planned to kill Rawson to get his hands on it. He knew Mrs. R. didn't eat fruit cake, and also knew she was addicted to a certain television program. So he waited until Rawson went out for his nightly pint, and—"

"I SEE CAKE poisoner Lee was given ten years today," Bell remarked to West, a few weeks later. "Mrs. Rawson was lucky you handled that job, Handsome."

"I don't know about that," West said, "but I do know that she and her husband have patched things up. I'm told they're like turtle doves. As for the investigation—well, you might say it was just a piece of cake!"

PREVENTIVE MURDER by C. B. Gilford

(Concluded from page 115)

"I was going to open the bottle and take a drink, Allan boy. And it sort of slipped out of my hand . . ."

He stooped for a closer, incredulous look. On the hard parquet floor there was a pool of escaped liquid, and broken glass. He picked up some of the pieces, fingered them, hot tears stinging his eyelids, blinding him.

Why hadn't he known there'd be more than one way for Rex to triumph? Why hadn't he known Rex would prefer the more violent

way—to smash, shatter, utterly annihilate?

As he rose to his feet again, he heard Rex laughing. All the frustrated fury of a lifetime welled up in him. In his right hand was the neck of the champagne bottle, its reverse end a dozen glass daggers.

He sprang, stabbing with the broken bottle again and again—stabbing at Rex's throat. And when he was finished, blood and champagne mingled together.

"Damn you, Rex," he said. "Damn you forever."

Your Turn to Die

by ELOISE COOPER PITTMAN

THE SECOND WARNING sent him to the telephone, feverishly dialing Hilldale's Police Station. "He's gonna kill me," he squawked into the mouthpiece. "Help me! He's gonna kill me—tonight!"

"Slow down, buddy," said the desk sergeant on the other end. "First—your name and address.

Al's cruel jokes short-circuited justice — until the crossed wires flared in a very deadly way.

•

Then—the rest. Just keep it simple—don't ramble. What's your name now, buddy?"

His tongue darted out to moisten fear-parched lips. "I'm Al—short for Aloysisus—Crump, Four forty-six Bayside, Apartment six. Second floor." He stopped to suck in a long breath like it was his last. The hand holding the receiver shook.

"And just who is threatening you?" the sergeant asked.

"I—I don't know. But it's set. Midnight, he says. You can't just let me die!" The sentence ended in a wail.

Al could hear the sergeant breathing over the silent wire. Then in a new tone, "Say, Crump, don't I know you? Ain't I heard your voice on the phone before?"

Al shifted the receiver to the other hand, but that hand shook, too, as if he had a hard chill. "Maybe," he said, deciding to play it cautious. "Maybe you heard it somewhere."

"What's this guy's beef against you?" the sergeant persisted.

"Why—why—" How could he explain and yet not reveal too much?

"Now, look . . ." the sergeant sounded out of patience. "What kind of fool do you take me for? Better explain, buddy, or I'll think you're some jerk trying to make the department look silly again. We've sure been pestered to death—" The voice broke off a second, then resumed. "Are you sure you haven't called headquarters in the past two or three days?"

Al was silent. He didn't want to end up in jail, but jail was better than—death. His nervous glance slid over to the door leading to the foyer. A movement there caught his attention. "Wait a minute," he said. "It's Western Union."

Crump ran over to the door and picked up the yellow envelope on the floor. Odd that the messenger would slip a telegram under the door, without ringing.

Trembling violently, he ripped open the envelope, then leaped back to the phone. "It's another warning—" Al's voice rose in a thin spiral of hysteria. "Tonight. It's gonna happen tonight. You've got to do something!"

"Sorry, buddy, if you do get killed we'll find out who did it. But we can't risk putting a tail on everybody who might have a persecution complex."

"You can throw me in jail. I'll take any kind of a plea. He can't kill me there!"

Al could hear the sergeant let his breath out in explosive gasps. "Say, I know who you are. You're the joker's been running headquarters crazy with those nutty pranks. And now the joke's on you, ain't it?"

Al glanced desperately around his living room, as if seeking escape and finding none. "Yes—

yes, I'm the one. But it's no joke now. He means to do it tonight, and I don't want to die!"

The sergeant ignored Al's hysterical plaint. "So you're the one," he said, "who's been running us around in circles—wives murdering husbands, only they didn't, and gas-filled rooms, only they wasn't. And all those phony orders called in to drug stores and supermarkets—and a load of sand dumped on somebody's front lawn. Takes a real nut to think such things are funny."

"All right, all right," Al cried. "So I'm the guy. It's your job to put me in jail. I deserve it, don't I?"

"You sure do, Al." There was a sneer in the sergeant's voice. "If you were an ordinary crook I'd have a cop out there before you could put the phone down. But what could we book *you* for? Being a public nuisance, or maybe disturbing the peace? Not worth the gas it'd take to come and get you."

"You—you're just going to let me die?"

"It's justice, ain't it?" The sergeant went on relentlessly. "No jury'd ever give you what you deserve." Then the line went dead.

Sweating, Crump jiggled the connection. All he heard was the dial tone. His fingers found the police number again. A different voice answered. He said the desk sergeant was out for a coke. Al

asked him to listen, went over his story again. The new voice said quietly, "Forget it, buster. Nobody would bother to kill a cockroach like you." There was a click in Al's ear, as the line went dead again.

Although Al's hands were slippery with sweat, he shivered as he cradled the receiver. The guy who'd threatened him meant business. There was no mistaking the grimness of the warning. Feverishly he rummaged around in his mind for a way to get action from the police. Maybe he ought to tell them about Anna Young's suicide last summer. Anna was eighteen, beautiful, and had no apparent reason for drowning herself in the Hilldale Lake. But Al knew why, although he hadn't meant it to end that way.

All he'd done was sneak a few home movies of Anna through a slit in the venetian blinds. Then he had sent the film to the Youngs. Well, why not? Her folks had the right to know just how far Anna and her fiance went when the kids were alone. Young girls like that needed protecting.

But Al hadn't been thinking solely about Anna's welfare. He was thinking about how Harvey Young's face would look when he saw the amateur flickers. Young was Al's boss, and had turned down more than one of Al's bright ideas. Maybe Young had tumbled that it was Al. Maybe it was

Young's voice he had heard on the phone.

Feverishly, Al dialed the ad agency and asked for Harvey Young. He talked through a handkerchief, applied for a job under a phony name. Then he listened to every nuance, every shading in Young's voice. Wearily, he replaced the receiver. Young's voice was not the one that had threatened him.

Then there was that woman who'd dropped dead over on Manchester Avenue. Thelma Griggs. He hadn't meant for her to die, either. But she'd keeled over the day she opened the package he'd sent—the one with the dead man's ear in it. How was he to know she had a weak heart? How was he to know anything about her? She was a complete stranger, a name he'd picked at random from the phone book.

The Griggs woman couldn't hurt him—she was dead. But she'd been listed as 'Mrs.' If he weren't scared to leave the apartment he'd look her up in the city directory at the public library—maybe she had a husband . . .

A moment later the phone rang. Startled out of his musings, Al picked up the receiver, listened for a second, then turned deathly pale. The phone fell from his hand with a harsh clatter. A terrible voice had warned, "Tonight —at midnight!"

Al's mind darted back to the time he'd started playing pranks in college. Other guys played them, too. But Al's jokes always stood out. Al's pranks had real imagination. It didn't bother him when the fellows hinted that maybe his brain was a little twisted. He knew better. He only wanted to have a little fun. Like Pa used to say—a little, harmless fun. Only when Al was a kid he didn't appreciate Pa's idea of fun. He'd been a serious kid, the butt of everybody's jokes. Always good for a laugh.

Take Pa now—he'd been a riot. Take the way he used to wake Al up of mornings. Sometimes he'd drag a straw across Al's lips, and Al would dream he was crawling with army ants. Other times Pa would hit him in the face with a wet towel. Or if he slept real sound, he got the hot foot. Then Pa would nearly die laughing. He'd get even with Pa someday, he'd vowed—when he got big enough to whip him.

But he never got big enough, nor strong enough. A heart murmur, the doctor said, and promised Al he might outgrow it in time.

Pa and Ma were both dead now. But Al tried to figure what Pa would have done to get the police on the job. Commit a real crime? How could he, and still stick to the apartment? Make a nuisance of himself? Shout the house down? That would only bring the manager, maybe get him an eviction notice. He liked this place—if he could live to enjoy it.

Set fire to the joint? Well, why not? Only that would be arson, and you could get twenty years on an arson rap. The fire idea appealed to him though. He liked the excitement of a fire, the hurry of hook and ladder trucks, the drama of the inhalator squad, the fire chief's siren, the sound of water squirting from the hose, the hiss of steam, and the chop of firemen's hatchets. There must be a way of staging a fire scene without actually having one. He'd turned in more than one false alarm—

There—he had it. A false alarm! But first, he'd plan—oh, so carefully.

Al looked nervously at the clock. Eleven p.m. He re-checked to make sure the door was securely locked. Then he put his plan into action. First, he built a fire in his metal waste-basket, and placed the basket near the window fronting the street. Then he went out into the corridor, and broke the glass in the fire-alarm box.

Minutes later, a dozen men in fire hats and slickers arrived. It took only seconds for the chief to discover that the alarm was a hoax and that Al was the culprit.

"You know what this means, don't you?" the chief asked grimly.

"Sure. You'll have me arrested. Okay. Call the cops!"

The chief looked puzzled as he dialed police headquarters. Al's attitude had given him a pronounced jolt.

At five minutes of midnight, the law arrived in the person of a plain-clothes man, a detective lieutenant in a trench coat. "I'll take over, Chief," the detective said. "There'll be no trouble. You see, he's anxious to be arrested."

The chief looked puzzled again, shook his head wearily and left.

The detective glanced at his watch. The muscles in his square jaw tightened as he stared at Al. "How does it feel to expect—murder at midnight?" he asked.

Al laughed. The sound was harsh, mirthless. "I sure outsmarted that guy on the phone, didn't I?"

The detective glanced at his watch again. "There's still time—"

The sick triumph went out of Al's eyes. "You're here to arrest me. How'd you know—" His face whitened, his mouth went slack as realization hit him.

"A couple of minutes to go yet," the detective said quietly, holding his wrist watch up to the light.

"That voice—" Al croaked. "It was you—you—" He started backing away, toward the door that led to the foyer.

The detective nodded. "I'm Griggs. Remember that name? Thelma Griggs?"

"But you're a cop—you're a—" Al's words died in a sudden choking in his throat.

"So I'm a cop. But a cop can be a husband, too. Thelma Griggs' husband. Too bad you didn't check the city directory and find out about me before you sent her that package."

"But how—" Al's teeth chattered so hard he could barely jerk the words out. "How'd you know —it was—me?"

"A guy like you has to brag a little," Griggs said. "Not about things that could get you in very serious trouble—but small deals. I've been checking for months in neighborhood bars, second-rate eating places, the only joints that'll tolerate scum like you. You weren't too hard to locate, but it took a while to make sure. My warnings were meant to bring you out in the open. Now I'm positive. You killed her—now you're going to die."

"But—but you can't, you wouldn't! A jury's supposed to decide!"

"No jury would ever give you all you deserve," the detective said as he pulled a gun out of his pocket and cocked it, very slowly and deliberately.

Al was numb now, exhausted from his fear. But his ferret mind was still trying to figure an out. He noticed that the fire chief had left the apartment door open. He began to run toward the foyer. "Look out, behind you!" he yelled.

"That trick's ancient," Griggs said, raising the gun. He let Al get to the door and then fired. Al spun around, crumpled on the foyer's terrazo floor. He lay still. His mouth hung slack.

"Okay, you can quit the clowning," Griggs said, easing forward. "All I wanted to do was scare hell out of you. How does it feel to be on the other end of a joke? You can get up now. I was only shooting blanks."

Al lay still.

Griggs turned him over, checked his pulse. "I'll be damned. His ticker must've been as bad as Thelma's."

A NEW COMPLETE MIKE SHAYNE NOVELET NEXT MONTH

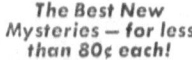

The Fiction House Press Replica Line is available at www.FictionHousePress.com